HAPPINESS

By Danielle Steel

Happiness • Palazzo • The Wedding Planner • Worthy Opponents • Without a Trace
The Whittiers • The High Notes • The Challenge • Suspects • Beautiful • High Stakes
Invisible • Flying Angels • The Butler • Complications • Nine Lives • Finding Ashley
The Affair • Neighbours • All That Glitters • Royal • Daddy's Girls • The Wedding Dress
The Numbers Game • Moral Compass • Spy • Child's Play • The Dark Side • Lost And Found
Blessing In Disguise • Silent Night • Turning Point • Beauchamp Hall • In His Father's Footsteps
The Good Fight • The Cast • Accidental Heroes • Fall From Grace • Past Perfect
Fairytale • The Right Time • The Duchess • Against All Odds • Dangerous Games
The Mistress • The Award • Rushing Waters • Magic • The Apartment
Property Of A Noblewoman • Blue • Precious Gifts • Undercover • Country
Prodigal Son • Pegasus • A Perfect Life • Power Play • Winners • First Sight
Until The End Of Time • The Sins Of The Mother • Friends Forever • Betrayal
Hotel Vendôme • Happy Birthday • 44 Charles Street • Legacy • Family Ties
Big Girl • Southern Lights • Matters Of The Heart • One Day At A Time
A Good Woman • Rogue • Honor Thyself • Amazing Grace • Bungalow 2
Sisters • H.R.H. • Coming Out • The House • Toxic Bachelors • Miracle
Impossible • Echoes • Second Chance • Ransom • Safe Harbour • Johnny Angel
Dating Game • Answered Prayers • Sunset In St. Tropez • The Cottage • The Kiss
Leap Of Faith • Lone Eagle • Journey • The House On Hope Street
The Wedding • Irresistible Forces • Granny Dan • Bittersweet
Mirror Image • The Klone And I • The Long Road Home • The Ghost
Special Delivery • The Ranch • Silent Honor • Malice • Five Days In Paris
Lightning • Wings • The Gift • Accident • Vanished • Mixed Blessings
Jewels • No Greater Love • Heartbeat • Message From Nam • Daddy • Star
Zoya • Kaleidoscope • Fine Things • Wanderlust • Secrets • Family Album
Full Circle • Changes • Thurston House • Crossings • Once In A Lifetime
A Perfect Stranger • Remembrance • Palomino • Love: *Poems* • The Ring
Loving • To Love Again • Summer's End • Season Of Passion • The Promise
Now And Forever • Passion's Promise • Going Home

Nonfiction
Expect a Miracle
Pure Joy: *The Dogs We Love*
A Gift Of Hope: *Helping the Homeless*
His Bright Light: *The Story of Nick Traina*

For Children
Pretty Minnie In Hollywood
Pretty Minnie In Paris

Danielle Steel

HAPPINESS

MACMILLAN

First published 2023 by Delacorte Press
an imprint of Random House
a division of Penguin Random House LLC, New York

First published in the UK 2023 by Macmillan
an imprint of Pan Macmillan
The Smithson, 6 Briset Street, London EC1M 5NR
EU representative: Macmillan Publishers Ireland Limited, 1st Floor,
The Liffey Trust Centre, 117–126 Sheriff Street Upper,
Dublin 1, D01 YC43
Associated companies throughout the world
www.panmacmillan.com

ISBN 978-1-5290-2247-6 HB
ISBN 978-1-5290-2248-3 TPB

1 3 5 7 9 8 6 4 2

A CIP catalogue record for this book is available from the British Library.

Typeset in Charter ITC by Palimpsest Book Production Ltd, Falkirk, Stirlingshire
Printed and bound by CPI Group (UK) Ltd, Croydon, CR0 4YY

MIX
Paper | Supporting
responsible forestry
FSC® C116313

Visit **www.panmacmillan.com** to read more about all our books
and to buy them. You will also find features, author interviews and
news of any author events, and you can sign up for e-newsletters
so that you're always first to hear about our new releases.

To my darling children,
Beatie, Trevor, Todd, Nick,
Samantha, Victoria, Vanessa,
Maxx, and Zara,

One of my greatest wishes for each of you
is that you will be happy.
Safe and blessed and fortunate,
and happy.

May you choose happiness
whenever you have the chance,
and cherish it as a gift.

With all my heart and love,

Mom / d.s.

HAPPINESS

Chapter 1

S abrina Brooks lay in bed with her eyes closed for a few minutes after she woke up, savoring the delicious limbo of being half asleep. She always woke up before the alarm went off at seven, and reached a hand out of the covers to turn it off before it rang. She rolled back slightly before getting up and she could feel the heavy form behind her, and hear gentle snoring as she opened her eyes, and saw the brilliantly sunny May morning. There was a mop of white hair in the bed next to her, and as she turned over fully, she could see the round black eyes open and look at her, and the wet black nose of her man-sized Old English Sheepdog, Winnie. It made her smile every morning when she saw him sleeping next to her, and tucked in beside her the tiny white, long-haired Chihuahua, Piglet, who opened her eyes, yawned and stretched. They were her constant companions in the converted barn in the Berkshire Mountains in Massachusetts, where she had lived for nine years.

Buying the barn and transforming it into her home had been her greatest reward and satisfaction nine years earlier, at thirty-nine. It was the result of the astonishing success of her second book. She had written her first book at thirty-seven, after a nomadic life and checkered career. She had resisted writing before that, because it seemed so mundane to follow in her father's footsteps.

Her father, Alastair Brooks, was English, and had written serious, respected biographies about famous British and American writers. She thought they were incredibly tedious and dreary, although painstakingly accurate. Alastair Brooks had a Master's in History and a Doctorate in Literature. He'd been educated at Oxford, the University of Edinburgh, and the Sorbonne, where he had taught for a few years before coming to the States to accept a position as an English Literature professor at Boston University. He had taught there for eighteen years, and died young, at fifty-one. Alastair had spent the last three years of his life in seclusion at a cabin in Vermont, where he moved after Sabrina had left for college at UCLA. He had dedicated himself entirely to his biographies then, with nothing else to distract him.

At her father's suggestion, Sabrina only visited him once

a year at Christmas, which he seemed to experience as more of an intrusion than a pleasure, but tolerated her for the two weeks she stayed. Once she left for college, her father informed her that she was an adult and shouldn't need much parental contact. She spent school vacations in LA and took a job in the summer for extra money. And as lonely as she was at times at school, she was never as lonely as she was at home with her father. She always suspected that he had contact with no other humans between her visits, except for bare necessities like the grocery store or the bookstore. He had no need for companionship and avoided it assiduously. Human contact always seemed painful for him, even with his daughter. She had never been able to bridge the gap between them, except when they spoke about one of his books, when he came alive momentarily, and then shut down again when the conversation ended. He seemed to exist only in relation to the historical literary figures he wrote about. The real people in his life were agony for him. He had been sent away to boarding school at Eton as early as they were willing to take him, as his older brother Rupert had been as well. Alastair had grown up without affection, and seldom saw his parents. Shortly after he'd arrived at Eton, when he was twelve, he had been brought home briefly for his mother's funeral and sent back to school immediately.

His brother, five years older, graduated shortly after their mother's death, and Alastair was alone at Eton after that. Having grown up without affection, he had no ability to receive it or express it later on in his life.

His childhood, his family, and his reason for leaving England were taboo subjects. Sabrina knew nothing about his family or early life, and he refused to discuss it with her. All she knew was that he had left England at twenty-six and completed his doctorate in Edinburgh, before moving to France and the Sorbonne. He had lived in Paris for three years, and met her mother there. She could only guess that his reason for leaving England was due to some sort of disagreement over his inheritance as a second son. His older brother had inherited everything, and Sabrina knew that once Alistair had left England, he never returned, and had never seen or spoken to his brother again. She knew only that her father's brother was named Rupert, and that he had inherited whatever money and property there was. Her father never went into detail about it, and never spoke of his own childhood.

She knew only a little more about his marriage to her mother, although that was a taboo subject too. He had met Simone Vernier in Paris when he was twenty-nine and she was twenty-one. She had been a model, and Sabrina remembered vaguely that she had been beautiful. They married a few months after they met, around the time he was offered the teaching position at Boston University. After they married, they left for the States. Sabrina had been born in Boston a year later when Alastair was thirty, and Simone was twenty-two.

The marriage had lasted for seven years, and when Sabrina was six, Simone left. Alastair had offered Sabrina no explanation as to why her mother went away, and made it clear that he wouldn't discuss it with her. She was never sure if it was her fault her mother went, since they never heard from her. When she was thirteen, Alistair explained to Sabrina that her mother had gone off with another man, and he had no idea where she was after that, or even if she was still alive, but he assumed she was, since she was very young.

If he had other women in his life, Sabrina wasn't aware of it. When he wasn't teaching, he was writing, and communication between them was limited. He maintained the taboo on subjects about his past until his dying day. He never explained why he had left England, or what had happened with the brother he hadn't seen since and had never communicated with again, and he steadfastly refused to talk about Sabrina's mother. Communication with other humans was painful for him. As she matured, Sabrina thought of him as emotionally paralyzed, and didn't expect anything more from him. To the succession of psychiatrists she'd had since college, and once she was successful, she referred to her childhood as The Ice Age. There was no way to scale the walls around her father, or chip through the ice he was frozen into, like some prehistoric man from ancient times they had found frozen in a cave. The distance her father imposed on her, and his icy personality, made Sabrina silent and shy as a child, always feeling unwelcome and out of place. It had taken her years to feel comfortable in her own skin after feeling so unwanted as a child.

Alastair had wanted Sabrina to attend college in the Boston area, at one of the excellent universities around them, but she had been hungry for warmer weather and people. She had only applied to schools in California, and was accepted by all of them. Alistair had had a rigorous study plan for her when she was growing up. He brought stacks of books home for her every week, and she dutifully read them all. Although he was unable to express affection toward her, he had fed, housed, and educated her adequately. He had cooked for her every night, and she ate in the kitchen alone. They lived in an apartment in Cambridge, and he had assigned her additional study projects. She had excellent grades, gave her father no trouble, and kept to herself, and as soon as she was accepted at UCLA, she left as quickly as she could, and their contact was reduced to her Christmas holiday. He had moved to Vermont by then, and in her junior year, when she came home for Christmas, he told her simply and directly that he had pancreatic cancer, and he was dying. He was surprised when she took the semester off and stayed with him. She was shocked by his illness, and she realized later that she was hoping to build some kind of emotional bridge to him before it was too late, but he continued to maintain his distance until the end. He spent his two final months frantically trying to finish his last book, which he did, and died two weeks later, without ever drawing closer to Sabrina. She waited for some final words of affection from him, but there were none. In his last days, he never spoke, and slept most of the time, eventually heavily dosed on morphine for the pain. There were no words for her when he died, as she sat quietly by his bed. She was twenty-one years old and alone. It was the loneliest feeling in the world. He had remained an inaccessible stranger all her life.

He had left her a little money, enough to provide a cushion to live on, and to complete her education. He was dutiful about his responsibilities, but never warm. She sold the cabin in Vermont, gave away his old, threadbare furniture and most of his books. She went through several boxes of papers in the garage, and found only a few photographs of him as a boy, with an older boy she assumed was his brother, but there was nothing written on the photographs. Whatever secrets he'd had he took with him to the grave. She found a box of her mother's modeling photographs, and she was as beautiful as Sabrina remembered her. Simone had raven-dark hair, and was tall and slim, with delicate features and big green eyes. Sabrina was blonde and blue-eyed like her father, with a small frame and delicate features, and looked younger than she was. Coupled with her shyness, she appeared almost childlike, even as an adult.

What Sabrina remembered most about her mother was her bright red lipstick. She couldn't remember any particular affection from her mother, who clearly hadn't been deeply attached to her, since she had left and never contacted Sabrina or Alastair again. She vanished into thin air after she disappeared. Alistair had received divorce papers in the mail afterwards, but nothing else from Simone. There had never been a letter or a postcard or a birthday card to her daughter, and Sabrina believed her father when he said he had no idea where she was. Sabrina had some illusions about her mother in her early teens and wanted to meet her one day, hoping she'd be warmer than her father, but had given the idea up as she got older. A woman who had evidenced so little interest in her daughter couldn't have been much of a mother, and clearly wasn't interested in meeting her as an adult.

Sabrina had learned to live without parental affection, or any affection at all, but unlike her father, she hungered for it. She envied classmates she saw with loving parents, and always felt like the odd one out. As she got older, she reached out to friends, who became the family to her that she had never had. She was a serious student in college, and her friends were almost like the siblings she didn't have. As a child she had led a very solitary life. Later, her shrinks agreed that she'd been love-starved. Her father had no ability to connect with other humans, which had been as much a tragedy for him as for her. Even when he was on his deathbed, she expected some sign of emotion, some indication that he loved her, and there was none. He lay in silence with his eyes closed until his final breath, while she prayed he wouldn't die so soon and leave her alone. He had remained an enigma and her mother a dim memory, a shadow figure in her life, who had abandoned her at six. It was heavy baggage to carry into her future when she went back to UCLA after he died, to make up the time she missed. She managed to do it over the summer and graduated on time with her class. She had no home to go back to, no relatives anywhere, except those in England she'd never met and knew nothing about.

After she graduated, she took a job at the Disney Studios as a production assistant, and eventually became a screen-writer, which was exciting for her. It was her first writing job, and she enjoyed it. She moved to Venice Beach, which was young and lively. She learned to surf, and was good at it, despite her small size. She was a strong swimmer, and met a young surfer from New Zealand on the beach. Jason Taylor was fun and good-looking. It was her first serious relationship. He had a job at a surf shop. Within six months he was at risk of being deported, and he asked her to marry him, for as long as necessary to get a green card. She was in love with him and didn't want him to leave, so it seemed a reasonable suggestion, and she married him. She had no parent to object to it. He had dropped out of school at seventeen and, other than surfing, they had no common interests. But it was exciting knowing that he cared for her, after years of her father's indifference.

The marriage lasted as long as it took to get his green card, almost two years, and by then, their feelings for each other had waned and there was little point to the relationship. He wanted to move to Hawaii to surf, which was of no interest to Sabrina. They filed for divorce, and Sabrina took a job in San Francisco, at Lucas Studios, which was a step up from her job at Disney. It was a great opportunity and challenged her writing skills, and she learned a lot. She started a new chapter of her life there. She had a few postcards from Jason after the divorce, and then lost track of him. He was living in Maui and said he loved it when she last heard from him. People had a way of slipping out of her life, without a trace, like her mother.

She was twenty-four when she moved to San Francisco. It was a fun city with lots of activity and young people. She loved her job working on scripts, dated a few men without any great interest, and at twenty-eight, she met a doctor, Tom Wilkins, who was ten years older than she was. He was handsome, brilliant, charming, and interested in all the same things she was. Fascinating and intelligent, he loved to read, loved films, had surfed in college, and went out on the waves with her a few times. He was almost too good to be true; an ER doctor with a specialty in trauma.

Their life together was full and exciting. Because of his erratic schedule, Tom had few friends, but their relationship was intense, and he and Sabrina were constantly together when they weren't working.

They moved in together after a year, and he was desperate to marry her, which she did at twenty-nine, at City Hall. Tom had no family and neither did she, and he never spoke about his past. All she knew was that he'd grown up in Chicago, was an only child like her, and that his parents were dead. They had much in common. From the moment she married him, he turned from Dr. Jekyll to Mr. Hyde, and controlled her every move, accused her of things she didn't do. Their marriage resembled the movie *Gaslight*. It was a nightmarish web. It took her five years to get free of Tom's control, which she finally did with the help of a group for abused women, and ultimately a safe house where she hid from him. It took her another year to recover and feel free and whole again. She had to leave San Francisco to escape him. Tom hunted her down wherever she was, and at thirty-five, divorced again, and feeling liberated, she moved to New York, to start her life over.

She had saved money from her job at Lucas, and with the money she had left from her father, she had enough to make the transition and move cross-country. Just as she had fled her father and the loneliness of her life with him, she headed east again, to New York, to flee the terrifying psychological abuse of her ex-husband. She felt as though she was always running away from something, but this time she had no choice. She had realized how dangerous and twisted Tom was, and she knew that if she stayed with him, it would destroy her. He might even kill her. He had manipulated her until she lost all faith in herself, and, once she got to New York, and as part of her recovery from her marriage, she started writing. This time she was no longer writing what she had to for her job. She discovered her own voice and wrote a terrifying psychological thriller, which was really about Tom.

She found a tiny apartment she loved in Soho, and a job as an assistant editor at *The New Yorker,* which was prestigious and interesting, and at night she wrote her thriller. She wrote it in three months, and spent another month refining it. It was a mesmerizing and frighteningly accurate portrait of a sociopath. She let her imagination run wild, and the result was brilliant.

She contacted an agent, Agnes Ackley, through one of her colleagues at *The New Yorker*. Agnes was tough and smart, recognized Sabrina's talent immediately, and accepted her as a client. The two women got on well. Agnes was in her mid-fifties. She sold the book in four months. It was a very respectable success, although not a bestseller, and for the first time, at thirty-seven, Sabrina felt solid on her feet and headed in the right direction. She didn't feel lost anymore. She had survived the worst and come through it whole. And with her writing, she was never lonely.

With two marriages behind her, and one of them to a sociopath, she had no interest in dating when she first moved to New York. Friends at the magazine eventually convinced her to try the dating sites on the internet, which felt dangerous to her. She was terrified of meeting a man who would turn out to be like the doctor she had divorced.

As soon as the book was published, the doctor tried to contact her again, but Sabrina's publisher shielded her, and Tom couldn't find out where she lived, and eventually stopped calling and texting her. She had kept the same phone number and finally blocked him.

Whenever she did read Tom's texts, he sounded as dangerous and seductive as ever, and just as sick. During their marriage he had tried to taunt her into suicide, and had nearly driven her to it. She couldn't imagine another human as dangerous as he was. It had taken her five years to feel brave enough to leave him, and find the escape route, and she didn't want to lose her way in those woods again, or any like them, with anyone like him.

Another junior editor at the magazine told her that the best way to get over a man was to meet another one, which sounded to Sabrina like curing the effects of one poison with another. Romance and dating seemed fraught with danger, but at thirty-eight, it seemed odd and a little sad to stay alone forever. She finally made a cautious attempt at internet dating, but saw danger signs in every email she read. She met a few candidates for coffee in public places, and they seemed to her either odd, tedious, or not too bright, with lackluster lives, and some were even boring. Only one or two seemed crazy to her, but most of all they were of no interest. Some of them had lied and were taller, shorter, or older than they had claimed. She suspected that one or two were married. Lying seemed to be a constant with several of them. She couldn't imagine meeting anyone she could care about, and she had met no appealing men at work. She wasn't desperate to meet a man, but it seemed like what she was "supposed" to do. After her isolated childhood, and her bad marriages, she was comfortable alone.

After discussing it with her latest shrink, and two friends at work, Sabrina decided to make more of an effort and went to see a matchmaker who came highly recommended. Dating appeared to be far more complicated than she expected it to be. Gone were the days when you met someone at school or work or through a friend, found them attractive, went to dinner, and fell in love. It was more like landing on the moon now, or attempting to refuel a rocket ship mid-flight in outer space. Highly technical and computerized, with algorithms, statistics, geography, and categories of desirability that had to match up. Chemistry was no longer relevant, and no one seemed to know people to introduce Sabrina to, and when they did, she wished they hadn't.

Sabrina paid the matchmaker an exorbitant amount for ten dates. She was a woman who had gone to Yale Law School and given up law for matchmaking because it was so lucrative. The men Sabrina met for a drink or coffee were stunningly inappropriate, with decent jobs that most of them were bored with. The age range she had opted for was forty to fifty; all of them were divorced, while many of them had children they complained about and ex-wives they hated, all of whom they claimed were crazy. Some of the dates were only trying to increase their existing stable of bed partners, while claiming to want a "relationship," which in fact was the farthest thing from their minds. She paid ten thousand dollars for the privilege of meeting them, a thousand dollars a date, which made it an expensive cup of coffee. She thought it was a worthwhile investment to pay homage to a biological clock she didn't actually hear ticking, since she had never wanted children, and didn't want to inflict a childhood as unhappy as her own on an unsuspecting child. She wasn't convinced that she'd be any better than her own parents at parenting. She had no experience with children and had never longed for one. Sabrina suspected a dog might suit her better and seem less frightening. You couldn't give a child away if it didn't work out, or stop seeing them, or divorce them. And her track record with her two marriages didn't encourage her, in terms of her own judgment.

After the tenth date arranged by the matchmaker, Sabrina made a decision to stop trying to meet the perfect mate. She thought that there was a good chance that a third attempt at marriage might be no more charmed than the first two, one of which had been foolish and harmless and a waste of time, a youthful mistake, and the second of which had nearly killed her. It seemed so much easier to be alone, and she had none of the frantic desperation other women had to meet a man. Her job and her writing seemed like enough, although she was embarrassed to admit it. It made her sound odd.

By the time Sabrina was nearly thirty-nine, she was sure she didn't want children. There was no appealing man of her dreams on the horizon, and she didn't want to go through the hormonal agony of freezing her eggs to save for a baby later, nor go to a sperm bank, which she thought served a useful purpose for women who were desperate for a baby before their time ran out. She couldn't imagine having a baby with a man she knew, let alone a stranger selected by a computer. She found the whole concept frightening, and remaining childless didn't frighten her at all. In fact, it sounded peaceful and comfortable to her, which set her apart from other women she knew, who were beginning to panic as they approached forty. She wasn't. She realized that she was a woman who didn't want or need children, and embraced it. She was busy writing her second book. It became an overnight bestseller. It was even more terrifying than the first one, and her readers loved it. She was making a career out of writing about twisted, disturbing people who did horrifying things, and she loved doing it. Her second book changed her life in ways she could never have imagined.

With the success of her second book, she was able to give up her job at *The New Yorker,* which wasn't a long-term goal, and write full-time. She had enjoyed her job, and the people she worked with, but she wanted to write her books without interruption or distraction, or having to go to an office to work for someone else. She bought a barn in the Berkshires and turned it into her dream home with a local architect, Steve Jones, and he and his wife Olivia became her closest friends. Sabrina was able to move to her new home in the

Berkshires before she turned forty, and she was never lonely once she did. The ideas flowed, and she had a home, a booming career, a life she loved, and money in the bank, and she had done it all on her own. No one was running her life or telling her what to do. No one was trying to hurt her. She had felt insignificant and unloved throughout her childhood. No one was rejecting, belittling, or tormenting her. She felt competent and capable. She had failed at the dating game and at marriage, but she was finally comfortable with herself, and had found the right path for herself with her books. Her life was full of the characters she invented, and the tortured lives she designed for them. Her own life had never been more peaceful, more fulfilled, or happier.

She met and enjoyed many of the locals, especially Steve and Olivia Jones, and she was a good sport about the odd single men they fixed her up with. They were almost as bad as the ones she had met through the matchmaker, or those from the internet. She had first (and last) dates with depressed widowers who missed their wives, men who hated their jobs, ex-wives, or children, or who wanted to have a slew of babies, which she didn't. Others couldn't keep a job, or didn't want to grow up, or wanted to control her and tell her everything she was doing wrong. She met commitment-phobics, and reassured them that she had no desire to be married either. There were a few nice men in the mix, but she had her life just the way she wanted it, and she didn't want to upset the balance it had taken her years to achieve. She had traveled a long, hard road to get here, ever since her mother had abandoned her at six. She had tried to fill the void her father left by ignoring her and being unable to love her. And she had questioned her own judgment after escaping her second husband.

Sabrina tried to explain to her friend Olivia that she wasn't a good candidate for dating or a relationship and was afraid to make another mistake. She didn't want to get hurt again, or disappoint someone, or hurt anyone. She was so happy with her life as it was; she had no desire to take a risk. She loved her life, and the wrong man might ruin everything. Dating just seemed too complicated and risky, and it apparently wasn't her strong suit. It was hard to explain that she really was happy. She worried at times that she was following in her father's footsteps, with her writing and winding up alone. But her father had been a deeply unhappy person, and she wasn't. She loved her life, her work, her friends, her home. It seemed greedy to her to want more. She didn't have a partner, but she had herself and the scars of the past had healed at last. What more could she want? And there was something blissfully comfortable about not being in love with anyone. She spent her fortieth birthday with a room full of good friends, less than a year after she'd moved to the

Berkshires. On her forty-fifth, she went skiing with friends in Vermont. At forty-eight, she had seven bestselling thrillers to her credit, and had made a name for herself.

She groaned every time Olivia came up with a new man in the area to introduce her to. She gave in occasionally, just to prove to Olivia and her husband Steve that she wasn't a complete hermit, and now and then they came up with someone decent she went out with more than once, and even slept with. But her heart wasn't engaged. She hadn't been in love since Tom, the monster she had married nearly twenty years before who had almost killed her, and there wasn't a single thing in her life she would have changed if she'd had a magic wand. She was a survivor and had turned her life into one that suited her and had made up for the past and her unhappy childhood.

Sabrina set down Winnie and Piglet's breakfast on the floor, and walked into her garden in the bright May sunshine. She had gotten Winnie the sheepdog eight years before, and Piglet the Chihuahua two years later. They were her constant companions. She was hoping to finish her new book in the next few days and couldn't wait for Agnes, her agent, to read it. Sabrina thought this one was even better than the others, and even scarier. In the end, her bad second marriage had spawned an entire career of terrifying books that people gobbled up like candy, and she loved writing. She just didn't want to live a story like it again, she only wanted to write those stories about sociopaths and serial killers and love gone wrong, with a fantastic twist at the end. Two of her books had been made into movies, and she was hoping for a series one of these days.

She checked her emails when she walked back into the kitchen, and saw that she had one from her publisher, asking her to call. She smiled at the dogs, patted both of them, and went to take a shower. She couldn't wait to get back to the book. Nothing else mattered when she was writing. She would call her publisher later. She knew it wouldn't be important. Probably a request for a book signing, or some detail about the paperback cover. Whatever it was could wait until she finished the book. She was humming as she stepped into the shower and Piglet chased Winnie down the stairs into the garden. As far as Sabrina was concerned, life didn't get better than this. And she was grateful every single day for how her life had turned out. She had worked hard to get here, and she was a happy woman.

Chapter 2

S abrina's editor at the publisher, Jane Madison, was a serious young woman who enjoyed working with Sabrina, although her books were so carefully vetted and meticulously researched when necessary that Jane had very little work to do on them. Sabrina disappeared for months at a time when she was writing. She wasn't a high-maintenance author, and didn't need or want attention. She called if a set of galley proofs was delayed, or about some technical detail, or the color of a cover. They hardly ever heard from her. She wrote her books and went about her business, and then her remarkable manuscripts appeared and became instant best-sellers as soon as they were published.

Jane's assistant Naomi answered the phone when Sabrina called. She was a pleasant older woman, and she enjoyed her rare contacts with Sabrina. She was a dog lover too, and Sabrina occasionally sent her a particularly cute photo of Winnie and Piglet, which Naomi always enjoyed.

It had taken Sabrina two days to return Jane's call, when she had a natural break in the book.

"How's the new book coming?" Naomi asked her.

"I'm in the home stretch," Sabrina said, tired, but satisfied with how it was going. "I think Jane emailed me a few days ago and asked me to call her. Is she in?"

"She's in a meeting," Naomi said. "Can she call you back?"

"Do you know what it's about? I want to get back to work." If Jane called after she did, she'd interrupt Sabrina's train of thought and it could take hours to get back into the book. She wanted to avoid that.

"I do know actually. We got a call from an attorney in London. He said that he's sending you an important letter and he wanted to be sure that we could reach you and would forward it to you. Jane said she'd let you know."

Sabrina couldn't imagine what it was about. She was published in England, but the attorney had contacted her American, not her British, publisher. She wondered if it was about a series or a movie. She'd love to do a British series. They were always so well done.

She hoped the letter wasn't about something unpleasant, someone claiming that her fictional story replicated their real life and she had "stolen their life story." She'd had a few crackpots who had written letters like that and threatened to sue her, but they usually ran out of steam and disappeared. Her books were so outrageously complicated that it was hard to imagine anyone's life being similar. She hoped not, for their sake.

"Did he say what the letter is about?"

"No, he didn't. He just said it was important. Jane promised to forward it to you. And actually," she hesitated for a minute as she looked over her shoulder at a table behind her, with assorted things they were sending to their authors, mostly corrected manuscripts, or galleys, "it came in yesterday. I was going to send it to you today."

"Why don't you just scan and email it to me?" Sabrina suggested. "Regular mail takes forever to get here. I don't know why he didn't email it to me at your office."

"Maybe it's confidential. And I didn't want to give him your address." The publishing firm kept a tight lockdown on their authors' security and personal information. They gave out no addresses or phone numbers or email addresses without their authors' permission. They protected them from stalkers and intrusions. Sabrina was hard to reach, and she wanted it that way. Tom, her insane second husband, still surfaced from time to time, usually when she published a new book. He was as crazy and sounded as dangerous as ever. He apparently read her books, had recognized himself in some, and still tried to make contact with her. She hadn't spoken to him in a dozen years, since the divorce, and didn't intend to. Jason, the surfer, had disappeared forever, with his green card. She occasionally wondered what had happened to him. It was odd having been married to someone for two years and never having contact with him again. But they were children then. It was twenty-six years ago. She hadn't heard from her mother in forty-two years, and had no desire to find her. She wasn't going to chase a mother who had left her at six, and never checked back in to see how she was. She didn't have any romantic illusions about her, or need to see her. Sabrina never thought about her mother anymore.

"I'll scan the letter to you as soon as we hang up," Naomi promised. Sabrina waited a few minutes and it didn't come, so she went back to the book, and forgot about the letter entirely until late afternoon, when she stopped to grab a bottle of cold water and feed the dogs their dinner. Winnie and Piglet had been looking pleadingly at her for the last half hour.

She fed them. They gobbled up their food, and then wandered out to her enclosed garden, where she knew they were safe. She stood in the doorway and watched them for a minute, as she drank the cold water. She was wearing shorts and a T-shirt, with sandals. Her long blonde hair was pulled back in a ponytail with two pencils stuck through it. She hadn't brushed it in two days. She never cared about how she looked when she was writing. She'd worked seven hours straight, without stopping for lunch, which was her style. She couldn't keep up the intensity and tension of the story if she stopped writing, so she rarely took meal breaks herself on time. She ate when she had a lull in the story or needed to consult her research or outline. She was just coming in from the garden when her friend Olivia called her.

She and Steve had grown up in Boston, and had taken refuge in the Berkshires when they'd found life in Boston too hectic. It had been a wonderful place to bring up their children, both of whom were now in college. Olivia was an artist. She had stopped painting when the kids were younger and had gotten serious about it again when they left. She painted beautiful landscapes and Sabrina had bought several of them from her. They'd been friends for nine years, since Sabrina had moved to the Berkshires and Steve had remodeled her barn.

Olivia and Steve were a solid couple and had a good marriage. Olivia was two years older than Sabrina and had just turned fifty, and Steve was a year older than his wife. He was one of the busiest architects in the area, and he had done a wonderful job with Sabrina's barn. It was beautiful and livable, and he had addressed every need she'd expressed, and every feature she had dreamt of. She couldn't imagine a prettier, more comfortable home.

"How's the book coming?" Olivia asked her. She was an attractive redhead with a good figure and did yoga every day. "How many people did you kill today?"

Sabrina laughed. "It's coming along. I have two more to kill in gory murders before the end."

"You're a ghoul," Olivia replied, but her fans loved Sabrina's books and couldn't get enough of them. Both her movies had been box office hits. "Hurry up and finish. I want to have you over for dinner. Steve is redoing a fabulous house for a widower from Savannah. He's a real southern gentleman, you'll love him." She never gave up, and Sabrina laughed at her. They hardly ever played that game anymore. Olivia had almost given up on her, but not entirely. She thought Sabrina was too content on her own and missing out.

"How old is he? Ninety?"

"Don't be such a drip. Sixty. Maybe sixty-five. He's very cultured. His wife was a famous British actress; they lived in London. She passed away a few months ago. He just moved here. I think you'd like him. He's on the short side, but he seems like a nice man."

"Terrific. Thanks. I'd better get back to work, before I lose the thread and the mood."

"You're always in the mood to murder some poor unsuspecting victim," Olivia teased her. "Call me as soon as you finish. I'll come hang out if you won't let me give a dinner for you."

"That sounds better. Talk to you in a couple of days."

As Sabrina started back to her office—the dogs had climbed onto the couch in the kitchen and were already half asleep after their dinner—she remembered the letter from the British lawyer and stopped at a laptop she kept in the kitchen, where she checked emails. She glanced at it and could see that there was one from her publisher. She opened it and saw the letter Naomi had scanned. It was longer than she'd expected, and she sat down to read it, slightly annoyed at the distraction that was keeping her from the book. But she was curious about the letter.

It was from an attorney named Grayson Abbott, from a law firm she'd never heard of in London. Her agent Agnes handled all her business in England, so Sabrina had no reason to know of the firm. The letter was very formal and polite. Her eyes opened wider as she read it, and then she read the opening lines again.

It opened with his regretting to inform her that her uncle, Lord Rupert Brooks, Viscount Cheltenham, had passed away several weeks earlier. The letter explained that her uncle was childless and without other heirs. The lawyer stated that after thorough research, before her uncle's death, in his final months, it was clear that Sabrina was his only living relative. Her uncle was the older brother of her father, Alastair Brooks, and had been the heir to the title, the estate, the manor, and surrounding land at the time of their father's death fifty-two years before. Their careful investigation had revealed that her father, Alastair Brooks, had died twenty-seven years earlier and Sabrina was his only surviving child, which left her as sole heir of Brooks Manor, its contents, and the entire estate and surrounding property, including the tenant farms, and the title which accompanied it. The attorney informed her that her uncle had left her a modest inheritance, along with a sufficient amount set aside to maintain the estate well into the future, and he had set up a separate account to pay the death taxes, so her inheritance should not be an encumbrance to her. The estate supported itself very efficiently, and all of the tenant farms were currently occupied and being farmed, in most cases by families who had been there for generations.

Grayson Abbott requested that she contact him as soon as possible so that he could transfer the deeds of ownership to her and handle the paperwork which was required and pay the death taxes. He assured her that all was in good order, but the transfer of documents should be handled as promptly as possible. He asked that she call him at her earliest convenience, and she glanced up from the laptop with a look of panic.

"Oh my God," she said out loud, and Winnie raised his head and looked at her. "That's ridiculous. That's not possible. What am I supposed to do with a manor, an estate, and a bunch of farms in England?" And why did her father never tell her about it? She knew nothing about where her father had grown up, only that he was English, and had a brother he had never spoken to again when he left home at twenty-six, after their father died. He had never mentioned that his brother was a lord, or what kind of property it was. She didn't need an estate in England, or even a title. This was completely nuts.

She called Olivia immediately and her hand was shaking as she held the phone. Olivia answered on the third ring and was surprised to hear from her.

"I thought you were working," she said.

"I was going to. I got ambushed."

"By whom?" She could hear that Sabrina sounded unnerved, which wasn't like her. She was usually calm and easygoing. She sounded rattled.

"I got a letter from a lawyer in England."

"Are they offering you a series?" She knew how badly Sabrina wanted one, and how she loved watching British series on TV when she wasn't writing.

"No, an estate," Sabrina said in a tight voice.

"What do you mean, 'an estate'?"

"Apparently, it's from my father's older brother, whom he didn't speak to, and whose name I only heard once or twice in my life, since my father refused to ever discuss his history or his childhood with me. His older brother inherited a family estate, along with a manor, a bunch of farms and a title. He just died, with no heirs, and by British law and tradition, he left it all to me. I just inherited a house in England and everything that goes with it. What the hell am I supposed to do with that? It's probably one of those crumbling ancient estates that was falling down around his ears and now I'm stuck with it." In her panic and astonishment, she had already forgotten that the letter stated that there was a fund to maintain the estate and that the property supported itself, which she didn't believe anyway. Her life was perfect just the way it was. She didn't want a property in England and all the headaches that would go with it.

"Holy shit, what are you going to do?" Olivia was as surprised as she was. "Will you move there?"

"Of course not. I'll sell it immediately. That's the last thing I need. I have a six-book contract, I don't have time to take care of some crumbling castle and run a bunch of farms in England. That's insane. I'm going to have the lawyer put it on the market right away, if I can even get rid of it. This is everything I don't want or need."

"Maybe it's pretty," Olivia said, trying to be positive about

it, although she agreed with Sabrina. It sounded like a headache to her, although the idea of it was vaguely romantic.

"My house here is perfect. I don't need a house in England."
Olivia didn't disagree with her, and after they hung up, she
went to tell Steve about it, as Sabrina sat in her kitchen, staring
into space, thinking about her father. How could he not tell
her anything about where and how he had grown up? She
knew when he had left England, though no details about the
feud with his brother. She knew that he had gone to Oxford,
the University of Edinburgh, and the Sorbonne, before coming
to the States. But she knew nothing else about him; nothing
about his family, or his childhood, or his childhood friends.
Everything about his past was unknown to her, and now his
brother Rupert had left everything to her, and she was sure
it would prove to be more of a burden than a gift. It reminded
her again how little she knew about her father, and even less
about her mother, because her father would never discuss that
with her either. She felt like a foundling who had fallen from
the sky without parents, and all she knew now was that she
had an uncle who had left her everything he had, including
a title she didn't know what to do with. She couldn't go to the
hardware store in town and suddenly call herself Lady Brooks,
or Viscountess. She felt silly at the very idea. She wondered
if you could refuse a title, and an estate.

She looked at her two dogs sound asleep on the couch

and tried to absorb what had just happened. She read the letter again several times, and then she went back to her office to work on the book, and her mind was blank when she tried to pick up the threads of the story. All she could think of was a crumbling castle in England. In her mind, it looked like "The Fall of the House of Usher," or something in a horror movie, like in her books.

She tried for two hours to get back to work and couldn't clear her mind enough to do so. She finally gave up, turned off the lights in her office, and went back to the kitchen. She poured herself a glass of wine and read the letter again. She knew it almost by heart by then. It was too late to call London, and had been when she first read the letter, but she planned to get up as early as possible and call the lawyer in London and tell him to sell the property. She wanted to get rid of it as soon as possible.

She had two more glasses of wine before she fell asleep on her bed with her clothes and the lights on. Since it was still early, she woke up at five A.M., which was perfect timing, since it was ten A.M. in London, and hopefully the attorney would be in his office where she could reach him.

She called the number on his letterhead after she made herself a cup of coffee. A clipped British voice had asked her to hold, and a minute later, a warm, friendly voice came on the line.

"Lady Brooks?" he said properly, and she winced. It made it seem all too real.

"This is Sabrina Brooks," she said, with the emphasis on her first name. "You can call me Sabrina."

"Thank you for calling me. We have quite a lot of paperwork to take care of, and I want to get started. What are your plans for the property? I realize it must be something of a surprise to inherit a whole estate, with a manor and a lake." He sounded young, and she wondered if he was.

"A lake?" Her voice was a high-pitched squeak. She didn't need a lake either. She didn't want any of it. Her father hadn't wanted it and now neither did she.

"It's a small lake, but your uncle kept it well stocked so people he knew could fish there. He used to let me fish there as a boy. He and my father were close friends. My father was very fond of him. He knew your father too, before he left."

"I didn't know anything about my uncle," Sabrina said, sounding a little lost. "I assumed he must have been dead, like my father. And I certainly didn't know about the estate and expect to inherit it," she said, sounding flustered again. "I can't run an estate in England. I live in Massachusetts, and I have work to do here," she said firmly, trying to convince herself as well as him that this just wasn't possible.

"I've read your books," Grayson Abbott said in a warm, friendly tone. "I enjoyed them very much. Couldn't you write them here, and go back and forth to both places? Are you married? Do you have children? The estate is a lovely place for kids. I grew up next door in the summers and on weekends."

"No, I don't have children or a husband," she said, as though he were trying to give her a child she might have inherited too. "I live alone with two dogs."

"They'll love it here." She had inherited six hundred acres. "What are your plans for the estate?" he asked her.

"I want to sell it immediately," she said, sounding more strident than she intended, and somewhat panicked.

"That would be a great shame." He seemed sad to hear it. "You should see it first."

"I can't. I'm too busy. I'm trying to finish a book."

"After the book then. Will it take long?"

"It wouldn't have. Now I'm not sure. This is very distracting."

"I can imagine. But it's a lovely place. You might love it."

"Even if I do, I can't manage an estate in England, living here. I lead a very simple, quiet life, I need that for my work."

"I think Brooks Manor would be an ideal place to write. I really do need you to come and take care of the paperwork. I can send it to you in the States, but it would be much simpler to do it all here." She was silent while she thought about it. Grayson Abbott was very persuasive, but all she wanted to do was get rid of this unexpected inheritance, sell it, and put the money in the bank.

"I need to think about it. I'll get back to you," she said nervously, thanked him, and hung up a few minutes later. If anything, she felt more jangled after talking to him than before. She felt like the boorish American who was ungratefully receiving an inheritance that she just wanted to get rid of. It panicked her to think of all the responsibility that went with it. She led a stress-free life and wanted to keep it that way.

It was a huge leap to suddenly go from knowing nothing about her father's past, to inheriting his ancestral home and property, as though it was perfectly normal. It made her angry at him for not preparing her for this, and if she had an uncle who had lived this long, why had her father deprived her of knowing him, and enjoying the benefits of a family she had never met and knew nothing about? Were they criminals? Monsters? Had they cheated or robbed him? Abused him as a child? What had they done that was so severe that he had never seen or spoken to his brother again? Thanks to her father, she had no history at all, from him, or her mother. She felt like an alien with no human history whatsoever. Other people had families and aunts and uncles, parents, siblings. She had had only her father, who was barely a father at all, and now she had no one, and nothing except a property in England she didn't want. Her initial reaction was anger at her father, and even a certain degree of fear, about what she was being pulled into. It was much more responsibility than she wanted.

She went back to bed for an hour, dozed, and then got up at six-thirty and went to her office to work on the book, and found she couldn't. All she could think of was her conversation with Grayson Abbott about how lovely the estate was, and the lake stocked with fish. Suddenly she was Lady Brooks and she owned a lake. She couldn't wrap her mind around it, and images of how she imagined the place kept interfering with the book she was trying to write.

She had written two pages by the end of the day. Inheriting her father's childhood home and finding out he wasn't who she thought he was had thrown her completely off balance. She thought he was a simple, modest professor, with good British manners and a solid education. She had never imagined that he was the second son of a British lord, brought up as an aristocrat in an ancestral home, and deprived of any inheritance because of the birth order and British law. She assumed that that was the feud that had divided the two brothers for the rest of their lives. Her father had never struck her as greedy. He and she had lived simply, and he was careful with money, but he had never deprived her of necessities, basic comforts, and a good education, "only" of affection.

The British system must have seemed so unfair to him, as it did to her, and now she was inheriting everything without ever having met her uncle. Her father had been deprived all his life, and now she would have it all, and didn't want it. The perversity of the universe seemed extreme.

She got nowhere with the book that day, and lay wide awake in bed all night. She called Grayson Abbott at six A.M.; eleven o'clock for him. His secretary said he was in a meeting, but he came on the line almost immediately once she gave her name.

"Sorry, Lady Brooks . . . sorry, Sabrina. I was in a partners' meeting. What can I do for you?" He sounded young; she wasn't sure how young, but young.

"I have to finish the book I'm working on," she said in a tone of desperation. "I just need a few more days, maybe a week, if I can clear my head. And then I'll come over and see the place." Part of her was curious to see where her father had grown up. The door had been thrown open wide to his past now, and she wanted to step across the threshold and look around. She wondered if it would give her some new insights into him, and his mysterious hidden past.

"I think that's the right thing to do. See it, and then make a decision about whether or not it fits into your life."

"I just didn't know anything about it. My father never spoke of his youth or his past. And suddenly I own a house, from an uncle I know nothing about. My father was a complete stranger to me in many ways. I know as little about him as I do about my uncle."

"That's not unusual for an Englishman," Grayson Abbott said kindly, "although he sounds a bit more extreme."

"He was," she assured him.

"He's been gone a long time, I see from the research to find you. He died very young." He sounded sympathetic.

"He did. He was fifty-one." His brother had lived to eighty-three. "Pancreatic cancer."

"And you were only twenty-one. Is your mother still alive?" he asked gently, trying to get a sense of her, and why she was so resistant to the inheritance.

"I don't know if she's alive." She was honest with him. "My mother left when I was six. I know even less about her. And suddenly I own an ancestral home in England. It really shocked me when I got your letter."

"I'll take you there myself when you come. My father lives right next door to the property. He and Lord Rupert grew up together and were close friends. My father is a year older than your uncle was, but in better shape. Lord Rupert led a bit of a wild life. He inherited just enough to spend the rest of his life on sporting pursuits, going to balls and parties, and having fun. Women were a big part of that." Rupert sounded like the exact opposite of her father.

"My father worked hard all his life," she said quietly. Their two lives had been so different, determined by destiny and their order of birth. "He was a professor of History and English Literature, and wrote biographies. He was an unhappy person, locked into a solitary world, a prison of his own making. In the end, he shut himself away completely to write. We were never close."

"Our British system can be cruel. I assume that's what drove them apart."

"It must have been. He never said. He never spoke of the past, and I never knew about the house or the estate."

"Well, it's yours now. I look forward to driving you there. Let me know when you're ready to come, and I'll be available. Maybe my father can fill you in on some family history. Good luck with your book in the meantime." He sounded upbeat and busy.

"Thank you."

Sabrina felt slightly more at peace about it when she hung up. But it was still hard to get back into the book. It felt as though so much had happened in a short time. She had been handed a piece of her own history that she had never guessed or suspected, which shed new light on her father, but still not enough. She knew now that he came from a titled, aristocratic background, but nothing about what had gone wrong to make him so disconnected.

It took her several days to hit her stride again with the book, and two weeks to finish it, but she was happy with the result when she did.

She called Grayson Abbott again the day after she finished the book. It was late afternoon for him. He was still in the office, and he sounded pleased to hear from her. She had made the hotel and flight reservations that morning. She was leaving the next day on an overnight flight and she would arrive the following morning. She had made a hotel reservation at Claridge's, where she had stayed when she did her first British book tour, and loved it. The venerable hotel was full of history and tradition, with impeccable service.

Grayson said he would meet her at her hotel the morning she arrived, and drive her to the estate. She called Agnes, her agent, after that and told her she was leaving, but was sending her the new manuscript before she left.

"I can't wait to read it. And since you're going to London, I think you should call your British publisher while you're there. It's good to stay in touch. How long are you staying?"

"I don't know. A crazy thing happened. I just inherited a house and some property there from an uncle I never met."

"Sounds like a book," Agnes said, and laughed.

"Not one of mine, unless the house is a crumbling relic, and the housekeeper is a serial killer," Sabrina said. "I guess

I'll stay a week or two, to sign all the papers and arrange to have it put on the market."

"You're not keeping it?"

"What would I do with an estate in England? I live in the Berkshires, that's enough for me."

"Wait till you see it before you decide. I can think of worse things than owning a historic house in England, unless it's a money pit or a headache you don't need."

Sabrina was pensive after she hung up. She looked at one of the Google sites for historic homes and found hers very quickly. It looked impressive in the photographs, and was definitely an imposing place. But there was no way to tell what kind of condition it was in, and there were no photographs of the interiors. She'd have to wait and see.

She had dinner with Steve and Olivia the night before she left. Steve volunteered to come over if she needed an architect to make changes to the house if she decided to keep it.

"I think all I need a real estate agent, but thanks, Steve." They wished her luck when she left and drove home to the barn. It was all the home she needed. She didn't need or want anything more.

She had sent her manuscript to Agnes that afternoon. Her bags were packed, and she had a dog sitter coming to stay with Winnie and Piglet. They had looked mournful ever since they saw her valises that afternoon. They knew what that meant and didn't like it, although she had hired a sitter they liked. She was due to arrive the next morning right after Sabrina left.

Sabrina had a feeling of trepidation as she got into the car that picked her up to go to the airport. Part of her was excited, and another part was scared. She had no idea what she'd find or what to expect. She was leaving the home she loved, going to one she didn't know, and no matter how "lovely" the attorney said it was, she wanted to sell it and come back to her simple life in the Berkshire Mountains and write her books. She didn't need or want more than that.

She could hear Winnie barking as they drove away, his deep resonant "woof, woof!" with Piglet's high squeak beside him, and she missed them already. All she wanted now was to see the property in England, make a fast, sensible decision, and get back here as quickly as she could to the place where she belonged. She had no need or desire for a title or an ancestral home in England. Lady Brooks? Ridiculous!

Chapter 3

S abrina slept for most of the flight to London, had a meal, and watched a movie for the rest. And as she rode in a taxi to the hotel, she realized that it had been three years since she'd been in London on her last British book tour. She was planning to call her British publisher while she was there this time, as she had promised Agnes she would. She had promised to text Olivia after she saw the house.

She had two hours to shower and change before her appointment with Grayson Abbott. She was meeting him in the lobby of her hotel. He had suggested a quick cup of tea while she signed some of the most urgent papers. They could take care of the rest later, but he needed to transfer the bank accounts to her name, and she had to sign some tax forms. Then he would drive her the two hours to the estate. He wanted to be there when she saw it, to make it easier for her.

She felt much calmer once she arrived in London. She'd been unnerved by it all before, and she realized now that no one could force her to do anything. If she didn't want the estate, she could sell it and no one could stop her. She was an adult, and she had no obligation to maintain the history of a family she had never belonged to. Her father had been an outcast in exile for exactly half his life. They were all strangers to her, her father almost as much as his brother, and she didn't have to keep the estate to please anyone. She felt calm and composed as she waited for the attorney in the lobby. She was going to take a quick look around the estate with him, make her decision, put it on the market to sell it, and go home. Even if she owned it now, Brooks Manor was not her home.

She had made no particular effort about her appearance to meet the attorney. She looked neat and clean, but she didn't dress up to go to the country, nor to impress him. This was a working visit, and she didn't know how much they'd climb around the house and on the grounds. She'd worn an old pair of running shoes, jeans, a T-shirt and a Levi's jacket. Her long blonde hair was pulled back in a ponytail and she had worn no makeup. She was carrying a big purse with a yellow legal pad in it, to make notes if she needed to, and printouts of some of the papers Grayson Abbott had emailed her, which she had read again thoroughly on the plane. She knew all the details of what her uncle had left her.

She was sitting in a chair in the lobby, at a small table, lost in thought, as she noticed a man walk hesitantly toward her, and seeing him snapped her out of her reverie. She didn't know who he was, but he didn't look like an attorney. He couldn't be Grayson Abbott. He was handsome enough to be a film star, and she spotted him immediately. He was wearing a perfectly cut tweed jacket, an open-collared shirt in Wedgwood blue, jeans, and black boots. His dark hair was immaculately trimmed, he had a handsome well-etched face, and there was a dusting of gray at his temples. He looked about forty, if that, barely more. He was so good-looking that she couldn't help staring at him, the way one looked at beautiful women. He glanced around the seating groups in the lobby. He was obviously meeting someone. She wondered who he was. He looked important, and totally at ease as he looked around and smiled at her. He had noticed her too. She smiled back, and much to her embarrassment, he headed toward her, which surprised her. She could feel her stomach tie in a knot as he did, and she was about to explain to him that she was meeting someone, thinking he was about to try to pick her up, although noon seemed early in the day for that.

"Lady Brooks?" She recognized his voice immediately, and before she could stop herself, she said, "Oh no." He seemed surprised and looked around then. Her "Oh no" had been because she hadn't expected him to be drop-dead gorgeous. She hadn't seen a man who looked like that and took her breath away since her horrendous ex-husband, Tom. She had come to the conclusion then that all men who were that good-looking were sociopaths, but there was no reason to believe that Grayson Abbott was. But being dazzled by his looks was a complication she didn't want or need.

She had come here to get rid of an inheritance she didn't want, not to fall for one of the handsomest men she'd ever seen. What had just happened had been precisely why she had never believed in online dating, which she considered a meat market without emotion or chemistry. Just seeing Grayson Abbott walk across the lobby toward her had flipped her stomach over. She didn't want to be attracted to him. This wasn't about him, and she didn't want her judgment clouded by an irresistibly handsome man. She needed a clear mind to make a wise decision, and the instant attraction she'd felt for him would ruin everything. She felt fifteen years old as she looked up at him from her seat. He appeared mildly confused when she denied who she was. He had been so sure it was her, and thought he recognized her from her books.

"No, no . . . I'm sorry, I mean yes," she said, fumbling with her words. "I meant yes, I'm just not used to the title." She tried to explain away her "Oh no," which referred only to his looks and how hard just seeing him had hit her. He was sexy as well as handsome, which was even worse. She hadn't seen anyone as attractive as he was in the twenty years since Tom. And he was even better-looking than Tom. She just hoped he wasn't a sociopath like him.

"I recognized you from the photo in your books," he said, and sat down. She seemed shy and nervous. She remembered then that she hadn't bothered to wear makeup, was wearing a T-shirt and the oldest running shoes she owned, and jeans with holes in the knees. This was a working visit for her, not a social event or a beauty contest, but now she was sitting with this gorgeous man, looking her worst.

"I hope not," she commented, as they shook hands. She dressed well and wore makeup for her book photos, although he thought the lack of makeup and chic clothes made her look younger than her age. A waiter approached, and they ordered tea. Grayson had a briefcase with him, pulled some papers out of it and set them on the table, and explained what they were. They were the papers he had mentioned before. She had already read them by email. He handed her a pen and she signed, was finished by the time the tea arrived, and handed the papers back to him.

"How was your flight?" he asked her with a warm smile, while she tried not to think about his looks and forced herself not to stare at him. It was silly. He was very good-looking, but so what? He was just a distraction.

"It was fine. I love London. It's nice to be here." She found herself glancing at his left hand and noticed that he wasn't wearing a wedding ring, which she considered good news, and scolded herself for it. He was apparently single. It was hard not to be affected by his looks. She saw others at nearby tables glance at him too. He was a very handsome man with a striking air of command about him, and when she called him Grayson, he told her to call him Gray. "That's a deal, if you don't call me Lady Brooks. Sabrina is fine."

"All right then. Shall we go?" They had both finished their tea, and they had a two-hour drive ahead of them to Hampshire. She thought it might be awkward riding in the car with him, and instead found that conversation flowed between them with ease. He told her funny stories about the property and her late uncle, whom he described as a Renaissance man, a womanizer, and a rogue. He spoke easily about his own boyhood, and his father. His mother had died in the past year, and he said his father was lonely without her. Gray was an only child and had been close to his parents, and still was to his father. He had had the kind of childhood she had longed for, and he seemed like a happy, well-balanced person; confident, at ease in his own skin, without being pompous. He said he loved his work and was a senior partner in the law firm. He mentioned that he had a son and a daughter. His son, Stewart, was twenty-eight, in Cape Town, South Africa, learning the wine industry, and his daughter, Prunella, Pru, was twenty-five, teaching in Australia. He never mentioned their mother, and without a wedding band, Sabrina assumed that he was divorced. He was fifty-two years old, and had read all her books before she inherited the property. He read them because he enjoyed them, and told her which ones he liked best. He was one of the most charming men she had ever met, as well as the best-looking, and he was easy to talk to. He didn't seem vain or narcissistic. He seemed perfectly normal, which Sabrina knew was incredibly rare, particularly with his looks. She had always found handsome men self-centered, spoiled, and difficult, and tried to avoid them. But she wasn't dating him. He was just the attorney for the estate.

The drive flew by, rolling along in his Range Rover, and they pulled up to the ancient historic gates of the Brooks estate in just under two hours. The entrance looked well kept, and the road was lined with beautiful old trees. They drove past the farms, which all seemed active and in good condition. There was livestock in the fields, men operating the farm machinery. There was a fork in the road and they drove to the left to the manor, and Sabrina could see the lake in the distance. It added to the picturesque look of the landscape. Gray was right. It was a beautiful place.

The manor house looked a little daunting at first, mostly because it was several centuries old, but the driveway was immaculate, the gardens impeccably tended. It looked like a home that had been well cared for and hadn't fallen into disrepair. Sabrina was quiet as she looked around, silently impressed. Gray could see it in her eyes. She looked very moved to be there, which was more than he had hoped for. He hated the idea of her selling it and the property falling into strange hands.

"Lord Rupert loved this place," he commented quietly, and it showed. An elderly housekeeper, Margaret, greeted Sabrina warmly, and said that she had known her father as a boy. She had only seen him a few times and she had been in her teens then, when she first started working at the house. Her father and grandfather had been among the tenant farmers, and she explained that her husband and sons still worked on their farm. She seemed very proud to be part of it. Sabrina knew from Gray that there was also an estate manager.

Margaret led them inside, where everything was in order and the house looked spotlessly clean. It was filled with antiques, and family portraits lined the halls. There were several large reception rooms and many bedrooms on the upper floors, more than Sabrina could count. Margaret explained that his lordship had loved to give house parties, and gave many, particularly during hunting season, although he hadn't entertained in the last few years, once he'd fallen ill. One could almost sense that some very lively times had been had there. Only some of the very old tapestries looked threadbare, while the rest of the furniture was in good shape and well maintained.

They spent an hour going through the house, and then Sabrina and Gray walked the grounds for a while, and at the end of the tour, Gray explained that he wanted to dash over to see his father nearby for a short visit. He said that Sabrina was welcome to come, or to wait for him at the manor.

"I'd like to come with you, if that's okay," she said shyly. She didn't want to intrude on him with his father, and Gray had already been so generous with his time and had spent half the day with her. He'd been an excellent tour guide all afternoon. But she wondered if he would have some stories about her father or the family history. "Will your father mind?" she asked cautiously. Gray laughed at the question. He had already told her on the drive there that his father was a retired judge. He had been Rupert's attorney before that, and when he became a judge, Gray had inherited Rupert as a client, and had been very fond of him.

"Mind? He'll never let you leave. He has no one to talk to now that Rupert and my mother are gone. He'll be thrilled to see you. I come here to see him as often as I can, but it's never as often as I should. I get busy at the office. I try to visit him at least every Sunday," he said with a guilty look.

It was a five-minute drive to the next property, and they drove up to a handsome house that was much smaller than the manor, but had a lovely, slightly more formal look.

"It was the dower house of my grandparents' much larger estate," Gray explained. "They lost their money after the First World War, as so many people did. They sold their estate and kept the dower house. The dower houses were for the widowed mothers of the current lords, once their fathers passed away and they inherited everything. As the estates began breaking up, and that style of life began to wind down, many times the dower houses were kept when the rest of the property was sold. My grandparents kept theirs when I was a boy. We came here for summers and weekends, and my parents modernized it and enlarged it once it was theirs. Then my father retired and they moved here from London, and he lives here now. It's full of my boyhood memories," he shared with her. He smiled at her as they got out of the car, and she followed him up the front steps, as he opened the door and led her into the main hall.

The house was elegantly decorated, with impressive British art by famous painters, and Phillip Abbott was waiting for them in the library. He stood up to greet them, leaning heavily on a cane but seeming otherwise robust, energetic, and alert, and his face broke into a broad smile. He was delighted to see them. He welcomed Sabrina warmly, and as soon as they sat down, the housekeeper brought in a heavy silver tray, for a proper tea with perfect little sandwiches; cucumber and watercress and egg salad and salmon, and a plate of freshly made scones with clotted cream and jam. Gray's father insisted that they eat well, and it was a full hour later when they regretfully told him they had to leave and get back to the city. Phillip looked wistful as Gray said it and he glanced at Sabrina.

"That was a bad business between your father and Rupert. I always regretted it for your father. I think Rupert did too, but he never admitted it. It wasn't in his nature to apologize or express regret."

"My father never talked about his brother for my entire life, and never told me why he left. Was it over the inheritance?" Sabrina asked him quietly. He knew the answers to her lifetime of unanswered questions.

"Not at all. Alastair knew how those things work. He didn't expect anything different. It was over a woman, Caragh . . . the name is Irish and means love. She was the loveliest girl you've ever seen. She and Alastair had been in love since they were children. Her parents had an estate near here, where she grew up. She and Alastair were going to marry, and then the boys' father died, and Rupert came back from South Africa to inherit. He'd been there for five or six years. He knew Caragh before, but she was barely more than a child when he left. She was a woman when he returned. She went mad for him the moment she saw him, and so did he for her. She was a beautiful girl. He was besotted with her. I don't think it had anything to do with the inheritance. Rupert was just a much more exciting man than your father, and he was clever about seducing young women and turning their heads, as he did Caragh's. Alastair was always an introvert, and Rupert was, well . . . Rupert. There was no one quite like him. He and Caragh ran off to Scotland and got married, a few weeks after he arrived. I think some terrible words were exchanged when they returned, and your father left. Caragh was an exceptionally beautiful girl, men went mad for her. She was Lady Caragh Ardsley in her own right. Her title was of higher rank than Rupert's; she didn't marry him for that, although he had more money. She was just a wild young thing, high-spirited and impulsive, and Alastair was always very quiet. She broke your father's heart. He never came home again, and he never forgave Rupert for marrying her. Three years after they were married, she died in a hunting accident. She fell off her horse and broke her neck and died. She was a daring rider. She's buried on the property near the lake. Rupert always stopped there. I thought Rupert would never recover, but he did. It took him a few years, but he came around. He never married again, it was all about fun after that, nothing serious. Every woman was fair game, nothing was sacred. Every married man in the county hated him. He didn't care. I think Caragh was the only girl he ever loved. She was a child compared to him. At least your father married later, in Paris, I was told, so he must have gotten over it. Married a French girl, I heard."

"I don't know if he loved her. She was a taboo subject too when I was growing up," Sabrina told them. "She left him for another man when I was six. We never heard from her again," and as she said it, she realized the crushing blow her mother leaving Alastair must have been. For a second time, he had been left for another man. After the first one, it must have been intolerable when Simone did it, and for the first time in her life, she felt sorry for him. His brother had taken the only thing that mattered to him. It explained why he had been withdrawn for the rest of his life and become a recluse in the end. Two heartbreaks of that magnitude must have been devastating for him, and she felt deep compassion for him. It was the first glimpse she'd ever had of his humanity and the enormous losses he had sustained. First Caragh, his childhood sweetheart, and then Simone. It made her wonder now if he had died so young of a broken heart.

"How awful for him," Sabrina said sadly.

"Awful when she died as well. Rupert told me years later that she was pregnant when she died. Alastair must have heard about her death. And Rupert was sorry when he heard your father died so young. Rupert told me. He read about it in some literary magazine. I think he wanted to contact you, but he felt too awkward after Alastair's reaction over Caragh, and thought you'd hate him. He outlived your father by nearly thirty years. I'm sorry that Rupert never met you. He would have loved you. No one loved beautiful women like your uncle. He could never resist them." He smiled a mischievous smile when he said it.

They left shortly after Phillip Abbott's revelations about Sabrina's father. She and Gray talked about it on the way back to London.

"He was such a sad man. He lived behind his walls. He never opened his heart to anyone, not even to me." Sabrina said about Alastair. "I suppose that's why, it wasn't about the inheritance at all. I always thought it was. I'm glad your father told me the story. I never knew anything about my father or his early life. I was never allowed to ask questions about his childhood or about my mother. It must have been a terrible shock for him when she left, to be abandoned twice for another man." Gray nodded, thinking about it.

He had told her as much as he could about the history of the house that afternoon, and so had his father. There were centuries to cover, and interesting stories to tell. It was a lot to share in a short time, and he could see that she had been moved by it, and by the story his father had told her about the girl her father had lost to his older brother. She had been the love of his life.

Gray wondered how Sabrina was feeling about the house now but was afraid to ask. He didn't want to press her, but he hated the thought of her selling it. She was nothing like what he had expected. He had expected a tough, businesslike American woman, who would only be interested in the property for its value, but he realized now that Sabrina's early life must have been complicated, with an unapproachable, remote father, and a mother who had abandoned her as a child. Something about her, her gentleness, her vulnerability, stirred deep feelings in him. They were emotions he didn't want to let himself feel. He wanted to protect her, but she was only there for a short time. There was no point getting attached to her. But there was something about her that awoke feelings in him he hadn't felt in years.

And she was thinking the same about him as they drove

back to the city. She was trying with all her might to resist him. Her attraction to him wasn't just about his looks. There was something about him, a deep well of emotion that she could sense more than see, and when their eyes met, she felt as though there were sparks and an electrical current between them. It took all her strength to resist him and try to ignore it, as she stared out the window, reminding herself that she would be leaving soon. Their thoughts echoed each other's, and so did the powerful attraction they both felt, which had no rhyme or reason but had hit them both like a tidal wave that afternoon. Sabrina was determined not to give in to it or acknowledge it. And her ancestral tie to the estate had affected her too.

"What do you think about the house now, Sabrina? Do you feel differently now that you've seen it?" he asked her cautiously. History and tradition were so important to him, and he wondered if they would be to her too.

"Yes, but not the way I expected to. I didn't think I'd have any attachment to it, but it's almost as if some part of me knows that that's my history, as though part of me belongs there. And the rest of me belongs somewhere else. I didn't grow up with all this or even know about it, but it's there somewhere deep within me." She sounded torn, which made sense, given her own history. "It's beautiful. You were right. But it doesn't make sense in my life now. Maybe if my father had come back here and we spent summers here, I'd feel differently."

"If you had, we'd have played together as kids," he said, wishing that that had happened, and that he had known her long ago. It seemed too late now for powerful emotions and changes in their lives. They were both on set paths and had been for years, with choices they had made. How would one ever change that now? And maybe it was too late for her to keep the house. He wished that just seeing it had convinced her to keep it, but he could tell it hadn't. He wasn't sure why, but he was disappointed by it.

"I don't really want to now, but I still think I should sell it. It just doesn't make sense for me."

"That's what you think. What do you *feel* about it?" It was the question she'd been asking herself.

"I feel attached to it in some way I don't understand and can't describe. I want it to have been part of my history, but it wasn't. My history is in a little apartment in Cambridge with my father, and the things I did as an adult. I've moved around a lot," she admitted to him. "I spent twelve years in California, for college and eight years after, before I came back to the East Coast and worked in New York for four years, until my books got successful, and then I moved to the Berkshire Mountains in Massachusetts. I'm happy there now. It really is where I belong. It's my home."

"Maybe you'd be happy here." He looked at her questioningly, and when their eyes met as he said it, they both had to look away. The intensity of the moment was too strong.

"I don't want to give up my mountains," Sabrina said softly, "or my barn. I live in an old barn I love with my two dogs." It sounded lonely to him, and sad.

"You could have both," he said just as softly, and she wondered if it was true. She had to remind herself that if she kept the house, he wasn't part of the deal. She was so attracted to him that it was confusing her, and she wasn't sure if she was thinking about the property she had inherited, or him. She had never felt as powerful an attraction to any man in her life, not even Tom. Gray looked distracted too when he dropped her off at her hotel.

"Let me know if you want to go back for another visit," he said, gently resting a hand on her shoulder. "I'll drive you anytime," he said, and she nodded. She wanted to see the house and the property again, but she wasn't sure now if she should go with him or alone. He waved as he drove away and she stood watching him, and then she walked into the hotel. She was more confused than ever and had no idea why she felt this way about a man she barely knew. It was as though just by being there all the powerful emotions of her lifetime had come bubbling up to the surface, and spilled everywhere the moment she saw him. What she felt defied words, and explanations, and even reason. It was all chemistry and instinct. They barely knew each other, but her soul had recognized a kindred spirit. She hadn't come to England for this. She had come to make a rational decision about a piece of property. There was nothing rational about what she was feeling. She had no idea what to do next, or more importantly, who Gray Abbott really was, and why it mattered to her so much.

Chapter 4

W hen she got back to the hotel at nearly seven o'clock, she called her British publisher, Felicity Parker-Smythe, as she had promised Agnes she would. Felicity was married to the CEO of a major oil company and had powerful political connections. They were very social and, as head of house of a major publisher, Felicity and her husband had a wide social circle of influential people, in business and the arts. She had invited Sabrina to a big party they'd given the last time she was there, on her book tour, and it had been a fascinating evening, with major literary figures, politicians, film people, and socialites all in one room. Sabrina had really enjoyed it, in contrast to the quiet life she led at home. It was the kind of scene one only came across in London, Paris, or New York.

Felicity was happy to hear from her, and Sabrina explained why she was there. Felicity was in her mid-fifties, with grown children, and her husband was both attractive and important. She had an exciting life, and was sophisticated and chic, and a powerful publisher. Sabrina's books did very well in England and were at the top of the bestseller lists.

"If you own a house here now, I hope that means we'll see more of you," she said enthusiastically. "That's a lovely area. Is the house in dreadful shape? We redid William's parents' house last year. I can give you some good names if you need them and have construction work to do."

"I haven't decided if I'm keeping it. I saw it for the first time today. It's a little old-fashioned, but it's in pretty good shape. There isn't a lot of work to do."

"Then you're very lucky, and you *must* keep it. You could have so much fun with it. So now you're Lady Brooks. My dear, how charming, we'll have to let your readers know. They'll love that!" It meant a lot more here than it did in America, where no one would care. Being a viscountess was not big news in the States, and if anything it would make Sabrina sound like a snob. In England it gave her new importance and appeal, and maybe even credibility. Felicity made it sound like fun. "You have to come to a party we're giving next week. It's a dinner for one of our big nonfiction authors, Lawrence Vance." Sabrina knew he wrote controversial political books, and it sounded interesting. "I'm doing it at the house. Dinner for eighty people. You have to come!"

"I'd love to." Sabrina jotted down the day and time, they chatted for a few more minutes, and Felicity told her how well her latest book was doing. Sabrina told her she had just finished a new one, and Felicity was delighted.

"See you next week! You don't have to be too dressy. You know how the political types are. Vance is a bit left-wing, so he's liable to show up in hiking boots and jeans, or tennis shoes and shorts. Very unconventional, so anything goes. I'm thinking black leather trousers with something sparkly on top. William hates evenings like that. He says he feels like an idiot in a suit, but he never wears anything else. See you Monday, and let me know if I can do anything to help you with the house, and you must keep it. We want to see more of you here!" she said, and they hung up.

Sabrina sat thinking about it for a minute. Felicity had added a new dimension to Sabrina's quandary about the house she had inherited. Was life handing her an exciting opportunity, while the dark side of her was pushing her to decline? Was she running away from it, as her father would have done, to hide in her barn in the Berkshires with her dogs? Was it an opportunity she should embrace and seize with both hands, or run from? A part of her wanted to keep it and open new doors and new horizons, and another part of her wanted to run away and go home to her secluded life. It was what her father had done when he retreated to the cabin in Vermont. She still felt torn. She looked at the room service menu. She was tired after the day of exploring the estate with Gray, and Olivia texted her while she was deciding what to eat.

"How was it? I can't stand the suspense. Call me," the text said, and Sabrina called her, and was happy to hear her voice. She felt far from home and wasn't even sure where home was anymore. She felt turned around. She was confused by her own emotions, and the exciting undercurrent she felt with Gray made it even more intense.

"Well?" Olivia asked her.

"It's beautiful, and I loved it," Sabrina said with a sigh, and stretched out on the bed while they talked.

"So you're keeping it?" Olivia asked, both happy for her friend and worried that Sabrina might decide to move away.

"I don't know. It's not me. The property is enormous. There are working farms, acres of land, and a lake. The house is very serious and old-fashioned, but weirdly it has a familiar feeling to it, as though I knew it in another life." She had felt that all day, and hadn't put words to it before. "It's big, and I don't know what I'd do here. It's all very English, and I'm American."

"It can't be that different," Olivia said comfortingly, which soothed her qualms a little. "You speak the language, for heaven's sake. And you'd do the same thing there you do here, write your weird, scary books that terrify your readers and they love it. You can do that anywhere. I don't see why you can't have both. Is the place a mess?"

"Not at all. It's in very good condition, though it could use a few modern conveniences, which is no big deal. Steve could fix that in a week. I just don't know if I belong here." Sabrina had been uprooted before and her home was important to her. She had to feel comfortable in her nest while she wrote. Brooks Manor wasn't cozy, but she had spotted a few places today, small rooms where she knew she could write, even a small study off the master bedroom that could be perfect for her to write in.

"Were the papers all in order?"

She hesitated before she answered, not sure if she should say more, or even if she could put what she felt into words, or should. "Yes."

"What are you not telling me?" Olivia knew her well. They knew all of each other's secrets, although neither of them had many. Olivia's life was an open book and she and Steve had a good marriage. She said there had been rough spots years before, when their kids were younger, but for the past ten years, everything had been smooth between them, for as long as Sabrina had known them. She couldn't imagine a better couple, and was impressed by how well they got along, and how considerate they were of each other. They were a role model for any married couple, the poster children for marital bliss.

"The lawyer who's handling the estate . . ." Sabrina started to say, and Olivia waited quietly for her to finish her sentence. "I can't explain it. He's incredibly handsome, and a nice guy. There's some kind of irresistible powerful electrical current between us. Maybe he's just a player. I don't know what it is, it's like being pulled into one of those currents you can't swim out of." And she had tried to stay out of it all day.

"Uh-oh," Olivia said. Sabrina had never said that to her before. "Is he single?"

"I think so. I'm pretty sure. He talked about his kids, who live in South Africa and Australia. He never mentioned a wife and isn't wearing a wedding ring. He has a single vibe."

"You might just want to double-check. How old is he?"

"Fifty-two."

"He sounds perfect. Grab him."

"It doesn't make sense unless I plan to spend time here, and I don't want that to influence my decision. I can't decide if I should embrace this and go with it or turn my back on it and walk away. I don't know if this is the right place for me," Sabrina said, feeling lost.

"It's the one you've been given, and it's an incredible opportunity, if it's not going to cost you a ton of money, and you say it's not," Olivia said. "Why can't you try it for a year, go back and forth between here and there, and if it doesn't work, then sell it later. You don't have to make the decision now." It sounded sensible to Sabrina, and she hadn't thought of deferring the decision. Olivia was right, she didn't have to decide right now, and it wouldn't cost her anything to wait. Just owning the place had felt threatening to her at first and she wanted to get rid of it when she first learned of the inheritance. But having seen it, now she wasn't sure. Maybe Olivia was right. "What about the guy?" Olivia was intrigued by that. It was the first man she had heard Sabrina be excited about in nine years.

"I'm not going to do anything about that. I'm only here for ten days or two weeks. That's a headache I don't need." Sabrina sounded firm, but the incredible pull she felt when she was with Gray said something else. "I found out today why my father left England and never spoke to his brother again."

"Over the inheritance?"

"No, over a woman. His brother married my father's child-hood sweetheart, the love of his life. He swept her off her feet when he came back when he inherited the estate and the title. They ran away and got married, and my father left and never forgave him. She died in a hunting accident three years later. But the two brothers never spoke again."

"How'd you find out? It sounds like a very romantic story."

"It is. Not the kind of thing I write, unless one of them killed her and cut her up into little pieces and buried her in a suitcase in the backyard," Sabrina said, laughing.

"You're a very sick person," Olivia said, "and you make money from it!"

"The lawyer's father was a boyhood friend of my uncle and my father. He knew the girl too. She and my father were younger than my uncle and the lawyer's father. My uncle had been away for years and when he came back, she had grown up. They fell crazy in love and ran off and got married. The lawyer's dad was closer to my uncle and the same age, but he told me the whole story. He lives on the property next door, and we had tea there today." It sounded like she was already entangled with the lawyer, more than she wanted to admit, but Olivia didn't comment. She didn't want to spoil anything or scare her friend off. She knew how skittish Sabrina was about men, ever since her last marriage, to the sociopathic doctor. She just hoped for Sabrina's sake that the lawyer was normal and turned out to be a nice guy. The property she had inherited could turn out to be a blessing of a lifetime, from what Olivia was hearing from her now, with Gray in the mix. She wondered if he had a girlfriend, or if he was unattached, but Sabrina was beautiful, impressive, and a wonderful woman. Olivia hoped he had the brains to see it despite her shyness, and the guts to pursue her despite the walls she had built around herself. Maybe spending time in England and adding a whole new dimension to her life would tear some of those walls down. Olivia wondered if that was what Sabrina was afraid of, and why she was hesitating about keeping the house in England. It felt safer running back to the Berkshires and hiding in her barn.

It was familiar. A whole new life in England wasn't, and it scared the hell out of her.

"It sounds like a sad story," Olivia said about her father's lost love.

"It is. I think it ruined his life. And my mother leaving him for another man must have been the final blow. It really is sad. I don't think he ever recovered, now that I know what happened to him. My uncle never remarried. He sounds like a big chaser and womanizer, from what the lawyer's father said, but everybody loved him. He had a fun life. He never had to work. And my poor father lived like a church mouse, teaching and writing his books. It's a shit system, but people seem to accept it here. It's the way things have always been. My British publisher is very excited that I have a title now. It's funny, that doesn't mean anything to me. I'm more concerned about owning the house and the farms. It seems like a lot of responsibility, just owning all that and making sure it runs smoothly, even with a manager. I'm afraid it'll distract me from my writing. I don't want to worry about a leaky roof halfway through a book."

"That could happen here too," Olivia reminded her.

"Not the way Steve built the barn. The manor is three hundred years old."

"You'd figure it out. There must be someone running it now. I'm sure your eighty-three-year-old uncle wasn't up on a ladder fixing the roof."

"I guess not." Sabrina laughed at the image. "There's an estate manager. I didn't meet him. He's away."

"So, what now?"

"I want to go back and look around by myself and see how I feel. It was harder to concentrate with Gray with me. I wasn't sure if I was falling for him or the house."

"I'd love to see this guy if he has you all turned around." Olivia had never heard Sabrina speak this way about any man. It sounded like destiny to Olivia.

"Maybe you will one day." Or maybe not. Sabrina had to make a decision about the house and the estate first.

After they hung up, Sabrina called the concierge and arranged for a rented car the next day. She was nervous about it, since she'd never driven on the other side of the road, but she wanted to be alone to explore the property, and she could get there with the GPS to guide her. She just had to be careful driving on the other side. She was lying on the bed thinking about it when she got a text from Gray, telling her how much he had enjoyed spending the day with her, and to let him know whenever she wanted to go back. She looked at the message for a long time before she answered, not sure what to say, and finally opted for polite and banal, rather than clever and flirtatious, which didn't seem appropriate so soon.

"I enjoyed it too. Thank you for making everything so easy, and I loved meeting your father. See you soon." All of it was true. She didn't want to play games with him or be coy. She was a direct, straightforward person, and out of practice dealing with a man on a personal level, particularly one she was attracted to. She had forgotten how to do that, and had always hated games. But she couldn't come right out and say that she was incredibly attracted to him, that he was the sexiest, best-looking guy she'd ever met. She smiled to herself thinking about how crazy it would be if she did.

She was surprised when he responded to her and told her that his father loved meeting her too. That time, she didn't respond, she let it rest.

She had a club sandwich for dinner and thought about her father. The saddest part of it was that the two women who had betrayed him had broken him and drained him of all feeling and emotion, so there had been nothing left for her. For the rest of his life, he must have focused on what he'd lost, and not on what he had. The one thing she knew was that she didn't want to be like him.

Sabrina was careful driving to Hampshire the next day. She tried to remain totally focused on the side of the road she was driving on, and not make any serious mistakes. The GPS got her there. It was a beautiful day, with warm spring weather, and it already felt familiar as she drove through the gates and past the farms. Margaret came out to meet her when she got to the house, and was surprised to see her.

"I just want to look around some more," Sabrina explained. "Everything was so new to me yesterday, I wanted to see it again." She felt like an intruder on the property she now owned.

"Of course," Margaret said with a warm smile. "Will your Ladyship be wanting lunch?" she asked, and Sabrina was startled by that again.

"No, no, I'm fine." She could get something to eat when she went back to the hotel. She didn't want to be waited on, she just wanted to look around, and see how she felt. The property seemed very peaceful in the quiet morning. She wandered through the house again and got a better sense of how many bedrooms there were. She counted twelve, divided between two floors, with an enormous master suite, a dressing room for herself, and a second one for a man in her life, if there ever was one. She checked out the little study she had noticed the day before, which had looked like it would make a good office. When she saw it again, it seemed perfect, and was within the master suite, so she could have privacy while she worked. There wasn't an enormous staff that she'd have to flee here, but there were a few people in the house: Margaret, a young helper to assist her, and a man who came to do heavy cleaning once a week. There was no longer a cook, but Sabrina didn't need one, and didn't want to be at the mercy of someone else's schedule when she was writing. She could fend for herself or skip meals, or Margaret could do simple meals, she told her. Meals had never been an important feature for Sabrina because they interfered with her writing and distracted her. The writing was more important to her. She had just proven that she didn't need a driver, since she had made it all the way from London in a rented car.

There were a number of gardeners and men who worked outdoors, whom she didn't need to be directly involved with. There were only three people who worked in the manor itself, which didn't seem like a lot in a house this size. Most of the house was unused, unless Sabrina decided to have a flood of houseguests, which wasn't her style.

If she kept the house, she'd invite Steve and Olivia to come and stay with her for a week or a few days, but she couldn't imagine anyone else. Sabrina was very private, and she wrote every day, and most people who didn't understand that would interfere with her writing. When that happened, it made her crawl out of her skin until she could get back to her computer. She was like an addict, having withdrawals if anything interfered with her writing. Olivia knew that about her, although most people didn't. Sabrina had a profound need to write every day, in some form or another, even if it was only letters, or an essay, but preferably a book she was working on. She allowed herself only a very brief break between books, and that would be no different in England or Massachusetts.

She realized too, when she thought about it, that her writing career, once she started writing the books, had begun after her divorce, when she'd left California and gone to New York. She had never been involved with a man while she was writing a book. She had no idea what it would be like to have someone in the house while she was writing. Someone who expected her to be present, come to meals or even cook them, keep him company and talk to him and listen to his problems, and make him tea and soup if he had a cold. She had never had to do any of that once her career writing books had begun.

She had done all of it for Tom when she was married to him, and spent hours every day fighting with him, and defending herself against his unfair accusations, such as his claims that she had had sex with a delivery man or a repairman or one of their friends. Their battles had eaten up hours of every day. She couldn't imagine living through that again, and with a normal man she wouldn't have to. But even a normal man would expect some portion of her time, and she was no longer sure that she could provide that for anyone. Ever since her divorce, her writing had become the priority. She didn't see how she could have a relationship and preserve that. Gray came to mind when she thought of it.

What would the expectations be of a man like him, who would want to go to movies, have dinner, watch a series on TV with her, or share a meal like civilized people, when she was in the middle of a book? It was something to think about as she fantasized about him. And even if some man agreed to it, he might actually find it hard to live with.

She didn't want an angry partner either, who felt short-changed by her career and the way she lived. Writing the books had been part of the healing process from the divorce for her, but it might be far less therapeutic for a relationship if she ever had one again. She couldn't see how to mesh the two worlds: life as a writer with a serious writing schedule, and life as a woman with a partner. If she had to choose, she knew the books would win. For her, writing was neither a hobby nor a job, it was a passion and a burning need. She had strong doubts that any man would put up with it. It was why she hadn't been unhappy being alone for the past twelve or thirteen years, because her writing filled her life and fed her soul, more than any human had so far.

She wondered as she had before if that made her like her father, unable to relate to other humans and fleeing from life, or if it was just the nature of how writers worked. She knew no one to ask and had no friends who were writers. Maybe the right man would understand, but she thought it unlikely. She didn't want to mislead anyone, suggesting that she would put her writing aside for them. She might at times, but it would take a very special man and a great deal of love for her to want to adjust her life for him. It was a serious consideration for her now that she felt drawn to someone, as she had to Gray the day before. What did that really mean? How could it work, and would it be worth the adjusting it would take? She wasn't sure. Having a real partner in her life, if it ever happened, would be all new to her. It was why the lesser beings and oddballs and eccentrics and sometimes outright jerks were of no interest to Sabrina. She wouldn't have changed anything in her life for any of them. And for Gray? He might be even more dangerous since the attraction between them was so strong it might eliminate everything else.

She was still thinking about it as she set out on a walk around the property. She had worn her old running shoes again, so she could go anywhere on the farm no matter how dusty or muddy or rocky the terrain.

She had a mission as she walked toward the lake at a brisk pace. She knew what she was looking for and she didn't see it at first. There was a clump of tall bushes that were six or seven feet tall, and as she reached them, she saw that they stood in a circle and there was an opening. She walked into it and there was a small clearing. It was bordered with rose-bushes, and there was a headstone. It was what she had been looking for. The headstone read "Lady Caragh Ardsley Brooks, Viscountess Cheltenham, Beloved wife of Lord Rupert Brooks," with an inscription chiseled below it: "My darling girl, sweet dreams until we meet again, with all my heart, R.B." Caragh had been twenty-eight years old when she died, and she had taken two men's hearts with her, and the baby of one of them. As Sabrina stood there amid the roses, she felt the enormity of the two men's love for Caragh and what her death had meant to them. She had been there for forty-nine years, half a century, and now she had them both with her. Rupert had been buried in the family cemetery on the estate, where generations of his ancestors had been buried for centuries, and Caragh was here alone in this quiet, secret place he had designed for her. Sabrina was sorry her father had never seen it, and grateful now that she had and knew the story. She walked out of the little hidden garden and was standing at the edge of the lake when her cell phone rang. She answered it. It was Gray. At the sound of his deep male voice, her heart gave a leap.

"Are you busy?" he asked her. He sounded just a little awkward, which made him sound even younger than he had the day before.

"No," she said simply. She was feeling subdued after standing in Caragh's private garden and thinking of her.

"Where are you?"

"At Brooks—more specifically, I'm standing at the edge of the lake." She smiled as she said it, and at his end, so did he.

"What are you doing there? Don't tell me you're going fishing," he said.

"No, I just visited Caragh's grave. I wanted to see it. Have you been there?"

"No, I never knew the story until yesterday. My father never told me."

"It's beautiful. It's a tribute to Rupert's love for her. She must have been an amazing girl."

"And maybe a bit of a wild one, like Rupert. I'd like to see it one day."

"It's inside a circle of tall bushes. There's a small opening you can walk through, right next to the lake."

"What are you doing there today?"

"I wanted to come back and see it quietly on my own."

"I would have taken you," he said gently, a hint of reproach in his voice. "Did you get a driver?"

"No, I drove myself."

"Were you all right?" He was surprised.

"I drove very slowly." She didn't like being dependent on anyone if she didn't have to be, and she didn't want to give that up, just because she was in England. If she was going to spend time here, if that's what she decided, she needed to be independent here too.

"I hope you're not putting a 'for sale' sign up," he teased her, and she laughed.

"Not yet. It's a beautiful day, and I'm enjoying being here. It's peaceful." But it wasn't lonely. One could sense activity and people around nearby. The farms were fully functioning, and everyone seemed to have a job to do. She liked that.

She was surprised that the decision about whether or not to keep the estate was harder than she'd anticipated. And as she learned little bits of history about the manor and her ancestors, she felt more attached to it. It was more than just an extensive property. Centuries of people had contributed their efforts to make it what it was today.

Gray loved hearing how engaged she was. She had an inquiring mind, she wanted to know more about everything, and she liked being involved in how things worked. She was full of life and energy, and having read her books, he understood her better now. Her mind was always going a million miles a minute and he was never bored talking to her. He had enjoyed her company thoroughly the day before, and his father had called him to comment on what a lovely woman she was. Phillip was only sorry that they hadn't found her sooner and that Rupert had never met her. He would have thoroughly approved of her and liked her too. It was comforting to Phillip Abbott to know that the Brooks estate would be in good hands. *If* she kept it, Gray had thought, but didn't share Sabrina's doubts with his father.

"When are you going back to town?" he asked her.

"In a little while." He had a spur-of-the-moment inspiration and reacted spontaneously. He wanted to see her and didn't know how much longer she'd be in England. He didn't want to waste any time.

"How about dinner tonight when you get back? Something casual, fun and easy; you don't have to get dressed up. I'd love to see you." Her heart gave a little leap again when he asked her. She didn't know if it was a smart thing to do. But she didn't care. She wanted to see him too.

"I'd love that. Thank you, Gray." His invitation also put to rest her initial concern about him. If he was inviting her to dinner at a fashionable, trendy restaurant, he was obviously single, which relieved her mind. She had never gotten involved with married men, and she didn't want to start now. That was one worry out of the way. Even talking to him on the phone, she felt the same irresistible pull she had felt the day before. It didn't make much sense, and she would probably end up selling the Brooks estate and would never see him again. But the prospect of having dinner with him was irresistible. He promised to pick her up at eight. She left the estate early enough to give her time to dress for him this time, and she smiled when she thought about it.

At his office desk, Gray was smiling too. It made as little sense to him as it did to her, but he found her just as irresistible, and the forces of attraction pulling them toward each other were the most powerful he had ever felt. She was a complication in his life he didn't need, but thinking about her, all he could do was smile, and throw caution to the winds.

Chapter 5

Gray picked Sabrina up at Claridge's promptly at eight o'clock. He was driving an Aston Martin, which he confessed was his most treasured possession. He had bought it for himself on his fiftieth birthday, and he looked sexy and elegant in a dark blue suit and white shirt. She had almost forgotten how handsome men looked in proper clothes. His suit was impeccably cut by his tailor; his shirt was by Hermès. He looked elegant and sophisticated, and he smiled when he saw her walk out of the hotel in a short black skirt and a white silk blouse, with her blonde hair in a French twist. She was wearing makeup, unlike the day before, and high black Louboutin heels. She didn't know if it was a date or just a friendly dinner, but it was fun to get dressed up and look chic for him. She never got a chance to do that in the Berkshires, and lived in jeans and sneakers. Dressing up in London reminded her of her old life in New York. It made her feel young and sexy and not just comfortable in country clothes. He watched her walking toward him and smiled broadly.

"Wow! You look incredible." She wanted to make up for her appearance the day before, and he looked delighted to see her. The conversation took off as fast as his car, and by the time they reached the small, fashionable Italian restaurant, they were talking and laughing, and he looked proud when he walked into the restaurant with her and tucked her hand into his arm. When they reached the table, he gave her a hug before they sat down, and she basked in the glow of his obvious appreciation. He had asked for a quiet corner table where they could talk, and they knew him at the restaurant. She wondered how often he went there with the women he dated. Just looking at him, it was obvious that he was quite a catch, and she was sure he didn't lack for women to go out with. But all his attention was focused on her, and he made her feel beautiful and appealing just being with him. He ordered champagne for them before they ordered dinner, and the evening began with a festive atmosphere. She felt the same powerful attraction to him that she had felt since she met him, and he seemed to be in the grips of the same feelings. They ordered dinner, and he reached across the table and touched her hand.

"You're going to break my heart if you sell the estate, you know. For a number of reasons. I'm sentimental about the place, and my father is too. But if you go back to your mountains in Massachusetts, I'll be sad if I don't see you again."

"I come to London for book tours," she said shyly. It had been so long since she'd been on a real date, she'd forgotten what it felt like with someone who one really liked and even cared about. They were holding hands across the table as she gazed at him.

"When was your last book tour?" he asked her.

"Two years ago," she said. He'd made his point. "I'm due for another one next year."

"I've known you for a day, and I'm already addicted to talking to you. I missed you today. Next time you go to the manor, I want to drive you." He was touched that she had gone to visit Caragh's grave, and he wanted to see it too now that he knew the story of the femme fatale both brothers had been in love with for their entire lives.

"I wanted to see how it felt going there on my own," she explained quietly.

"And how was it?"

"It felt good, almost like home."

"What's it going to take to make you fall in love with it and decide to keep it?" he asked with a hopeful look. He wanted to see more of her and get to know her. He had already added a new dimension to her life, that of being a woman with a man she really liked, which she had avoided for so long and had told herself she didn't care about. Now she did.

"Maybe I need a little more time to think about it and get used to the idea. I've never thought about dividing my time between the States and Europe. It's a luxury having two homes." But the fact that the Brooks estate would support itself was a strong point in its favor. She still had to adjust to the concept in order to justify it to herself.

"You deserve it, Sabrina," he said seriously. "And you're fortunate that you can take your work with you."

"That's true." She nodded. "I've always told myself I wanted a simple life, a real one that didn't include owning an estate in England, and my own lake." She grinned at him and he laughed. "Where did you grow up?" she asked him.

"Here in London. Boarding school, the usual, law school. I spent summers in the country, playing on the estate you now own. I had a very mundane British upper-middle-class upbringing, became a lawyer, and went to work for my father's law firm, and I enjoy what I do. How did you start writing those terrifying books?" he asked her, intrigued by her career and how successful she was.

"I married a lunatic, and I've been writing about him, and people like him, ever since." She was smiling as she said it and kept it light. She didn't give him any of the details of her traumatic second marriage. There was no need to, and she never talked about it. "I have fun with it."

"You don't have children, do you?" he asked, curious about her. She seemed like such a strong, straightforward person, and he loved that about her. She was honest and uncomplicated, and said what she thought without being harsh. He liked how gentle and feminine she was. He already knew that her parents had been difficult, and he could guess that she hadn't had an easy childhood, with a severely damaged father, emotionally, and a mother who had abandoned her, but there was no trace of it in her attitudes or what she spoke about. And no bitterness about her past.

"I didn't think I'd be good at mothering," she said, about children.

"I doubt that, but they grow up so quickly, they're only yours for such a short time. I hardly see mine anymore, living in Australia and South Africa. I miss them, but they need their own lives. I call them frequently, but they're busy, as they should be. What was it like making the movies of your books?" he asked, changing the subject. She told him about it, and had him laughing at the countless crazy incidents that had happened on the set.

"I want to do a series now, that would really be fun, and challenging to keep it going for several seasons." Professionally, she had a full, busy life, and she seemed to take her success in stride and was very modest about it. He liked that about her too. She didn't show off, and was very discreet, which impressed him. He didn't feel like she wanted to compete with him. He had never met anyone like her. He was an avid sailor, and they talked about that too over dinner, and she told him about her years surfing in Venice Beach when she had worked for Disney. She didn't tell him about the surfer from New Zealand she had married so he could get his green card. It seemed so foolish now in retrospect. He didn't need to know that about her yet, and she didn't offer details about the anguish she'd suffered with her second husband. She usually glossed over it if she mentioned it at all. She preferred to keep things light, and her marriages were a long time ago now. They were the distant past, not her everyday life. He didn't mention his, which she thought was discreet of him. It had obviously not been a happy marriage or he wouldn't be on his own now, having dinner with her. And she could tell that he was the kind of man who would tell her if he was married. He was clearly an upstanding guy. And she liked that he didn't complain about his ex-wife.

The evening passed too quickly. They stretched it a little longer with drinks at the bar at Claridge's when he brought her back. They clearly didn't want to leave each other, and despite the powerful attraction they both felt, she didn't want to invite him upstairs, and he didn't ask. It was too soon, and it would have spoiled everything if they made it just about sex. There seemed to be a lot more between them, which she wanted to explore with caution, and savor the discoveries, at least while she was in London, even if it went no further after she left.

If she kept the estate and spent time there, they would have the luxury of time to be together. She didn't want to rush it. He could tell by what she said, and her actions, and he respected her for it, and followed her lead on that. She was a woman one could only respect and cherish, and he hoped he would have the opportunity to get to know her better, although he didn't know when or where or how. It was bad luck for both of them that they lived three thousand miles apart, but if it was meant to be, destiny would have a hand in it, and they would work it out. For now, they had shared a delicious evening, enjoying each moment together, and it was one-thirty in the morning when he walked her into the lobby, kissed her on the cheek, and left her at the elevator.

She was still smiling when she got to her room. He was the most appealing man she'd ever met. Tender, kind, funny, and smart, he had a great sense of humor and she could tell he had a good heart. He was from an eminently respectable background and had a successful career. He wasn't crazy, angry, neurotic, demented, or bitter, didn't hate his parents, and wasn't angry at the world or politically weird like every other man she'd ever gone out with or been fixed up with. But she still didn't want her decision about the Brooks estate to rest on a possible romance with Gray. That had to remain a separate issue. She had to make that decision based on whether or not it made sense in her life, not on a relationship she hoped to have that might never happen.

He sent her a text while she was getting undressed. "Best evening I've had in years. Thank you. Hope to see you this weekend." She smiled as she read it and answered quickly.

"Wonderful. Thank you. Sleep tight." There was a growing intimacy between them that she loved.

He texted her from his garage, turned off the car, and let himself into the house. He saw that the housekeeper had left the light on in the kitchen. He was distracted, thinking about Sabrina, and was serious as he thought about her. He hadn't been as attracted to any woman in years, maybe ever, and wanted to have a serious conversation with her, but he had just met her, and it was too soon.

He heard a noise in the kitchen as he let himself into the house, and hoped it wasn't a burglar. He hadn't put the alarm on and the housekeeper never did when he was in town. He grabbed a poker from the fireplace, advanced into the kitchen silently with the poker raised, and found himself staring at a small woman in jeans and a sweatshirt, with short tousled gray hair and a lined face, and she looked as surprised as he did when she saw him with the poker and his arm raised. She didn't look frightened or pleased to see him, as he lowered his arm with a look of surprise.

"You're back. I didn't know you were coming home this soon," he said, and didn't come any closer, and she made no move toward him. She had made herself toast and a cup of tea.

"Pru was going on holiday with friends, to New Zealand, so there was no point staying. I stopped to see a friend in New Delhi on the way back, and I just got in an hour ago." She didn't ask him where he'd been, and he didn't ask who the friend in New Delhi was. They had been living separate lives for the past ten years, and with the children gone, they no longer made any pretense. Their relationship wasn't bitter or angry or hostile, it was nonexistent. They were polite to each other, although their relationship wasn't warm. They had made no agreements. They had simply drifted apart for years, until there was no longer any bond between them. They were roommates living under one roof, with separate lives, separate friends, separate interests. They had a silent understanding. They were married in name only. He knew she'd had an affair with a married friend of theirs for several years, and had guessed that it was over. There had been others. He had had brief affairs with several women too. But there was no one he had ever cared enough about to want to negotiate a major change with her, and she appeared to feel that way too. Once in a while they went out together to some event they were both invited to, but they both preferred keeping their lives separate. They kept up appearances, for the children and their social circle, but the arrangement had gotten more and more distant over the years.

Matilda traveled most of the time now. He knew she'd been visiting their daughter in Sydney, and she had friends in Paris she visited frequently. She hadn't worked in years, since before the children were born, so she was free to do what she wanted now, and he was content to live alone when she was gone. He almost forgot that he was married sometimes. It didn't matter, except now it did, and he wanted to tell Sabrina, but he hadn't wanted to spoil the evening with her. It needed to be said, and he already cared enough about her to want to tell her the truth, as soon as the right moment came to do so. He wasn't sure how well she'd take the news. Americans weren't as given to the kind of arrangements people made in Europe when their marriages weren't working. In Europe, unhappy couples had the kind of arrangements he and Matilda had had for years. Americans were more likely to pay the piper and get divorced, and divide their assets accordingly. Most of the men Gray knew didn't get divorced unless they met someone they wanted to marry, and until then it was less costly and more practical to support one household than two, which was the unspoken agreement he and Matilda had. It had worked adequately for the last ten years. But with a woman like Sabrina, he wanted to be honest and tell her, before things went any further. He could feel them heading in a serious direction, and at some point, the tidal wave of their feelings for each other would be hard to stop. He wanted her to know before that. He'd been thinking about it all day, even at dinner. He wanted to choose the right moment, but she wasn't the kind of woman he wanted to lie to or omit the facts of his situation to. Most people knew that he was married, so it didn't require an explanation, but Sabrina didn't know, and he wanted to make it clear to her, and explain the state his marriage was in. He dreaded telling her, and he knew he had to, but their evening together had been too perfect. He didn't want to spoil it, so he'd put it off.

"How long are you in town for?" Gray asked his wife as she put her cup in the sink.

"I don't know. I've only been home for an hour. I'm thinking about going to Istanbul with some friends, or Rome, but probably not for a few weeks. Is there a problem?"

"No. Just curious. How's Pru?" he asked about their daughter. The children were all they had in common now.

"She's fine. She has a new boss she hates, and a new boyfriend, who's quite dishy. I don't think it will last long. She's not taking it too seriously."

"That's good," Gray said. Pru was still young. Their daughter wouldn't be home again until Christmas, which seemed like an eternity to him. Matilda had been with her for three weeks, since there was nothing pressing for her to do in London, which was why she traveled so much. She had a very pleasant life, which he provided for her. They had married so young they'd had no idea what they were getting into, and how little they would have in common within a few years. Their relationship had disintegrated rapidly, and they'd stayed together for the children. Now there was no excuse, except that it would be complicated and costly to unravel, and it was easier and less expensive like this.

There had been no major reason for either of them to ask for a divorce. There had never been a divorce in either of their families, and Gray had no desire to be the first, nor did Matilda. Matilda's two sisters had similar arrangements with their husbands, and occasionally the three sisters traveled together. One of their husbands had a mistress and had recently had a baby with her, which seemed beyond the pale to Matilda, and Gray agreed with her. Once it reached the point of having hidden secret families, Gray thought divorce would be preferable. He and Matilda weren't in that situation, fortunately.

But with Sabrina's arrival on the scene, there was no telling what might happen. Everything about her and what he felt for her was different, and he wanted her to know about Matilda as soon as possible. He should have told her the day before when they went to the Brooks estate, but he had been so bowled over by her, he just couldn't bring himself to tell her and spoil everything, and the same had been true tonight at the restaurant. He might tell her over the weekend. Having Matilda home didn't change his freedom to go out with her. He and Matilda never spent time together.

He said "Welcome back" over his shoulder and went upstairs to his own room. He was lost in thought, thinking about Sabrina, and the evening they had just spent together. It really had been perfect. She was an amazing woman.

He heard Matilda's door close a few minutes later. Sometimes it really was hard to remember that he was married. It just didn't feel like he was anymore, and hadn't in years. They were roommates now, and nothing more.

Sabrina rented a car again on Saturday morning. She had spoken to Margaret, the housekeeper, about it when she'd been there. She wanted to spend the night in the manor and see how she felt there. She left Claridge's early, drove to the estate, and was there by ten-thirty. Gray surprised her and called her at eleven.

"I hope I didn't wake you," he said, concerned.

"No, I've been up for hours."

"Are you out and about?"

"I'm at the estate. I drove here this morning."

"I can't keep track of you," he said. "I have a few more bank papers for you to sign. Nothing urgent. I'm coming to see my father this afternoon. Could I drop by then? The papers are purely an excuse," he pointed out to her. "I want to see you. I had such a lovely time with you the other night."

"So did I," she said, smiling. "And of course you can come over. Would you like to stay for dinner?"

"I'd love to. I'll bring the wine."

They were both pleased with the plan and looking forward to it. Sabrina was excited all day, knowing she was going to see him. She rode one of the two horses they had in the stable. They were quite docile, and she took one of the grooms with her to show her the trails she could ride safely. She was just coming home when Gray arrived, after his visit to his father. The groom helped her dismount and led the horse away after Sabrina thanked him. She'd ridden for two hours and enjoyed it. Gray was impressed by her once again. She was a proficient rider, although she said she didn't ride often. She and Steve and Olivia rode occasionally in the Berkshires, but the trails she'd been on that afternoon were much prettier. It was a nice way to tour the estate, and she had a better sense of what was there now, since it was her third visit to the property, and this would be the first time she was going to spend the night. Gray was impressed by that too. She was trying to get a thorough impression of how she felt there before she made a final decision about whether to keep the estate.

They covered a dozen subjects while she put dinner together from what Margaret had left behind. Gray was tempted to say something to her about Matilda before they ate, and then put it off until after. There was no good time to upset her, and he hated to spoil her first weekend in her new home. He had a strong suspicion that she was going to be seriously upset, and he hated to be the one to upset her, and wished he had told her sooner, when they met. Their mutual attraction might have overcome it anyway. He was only three days late telling her, but it felt like a long time to him. They were moving swiftly, swept along by the chemistry between them, which seemed to get stronger each time they met. There was nothing to stop them, except a desire to be somewhat sensible, but there were no obstacles that Sabrina knew of, and Gray didn't think there were any on her side. She would have said something if she had a boyfriend. In fact, she had mentioned more than once that she was alone at home. The only obstacle they had to any kind of serious involvement, if that was what they wanted, was Matilda, and Sabrina didn't know about her yet.

They had a cozy dinner in the manor kitchen. Margaret and her assistant had gone home, and Sabrina put together a very decent meal of roast chicken and vegetables from the garden. He relaxed as he sat in the kitchen with her, and they took a walk to the lake after dinner. It was still light out, and the air was balmy. She showed him Caragh's monument, which he had never seen before, and they were both touched by it. As they stood in the secluded rose garden, he put his arms around her and kissed her. Nothing could have stopped him, and Sabrina didn't want to. He held her after they kissed, as though it was the most natural thing in the world, and he felt as though he had been waiting for her all his life. They stopped and kissed several times on the way back. They walked back hand in hand, with comfortable silences between them, and a few words from time to time. They were totally at ease with each other. Their meeting seemed magical and providential. And there was no way he could tell her about Matilda after that. Not that night. He wanted to revel in the moment with her.

They didn't go to bed with each other that night. Sabrina was still trying to be sensible, and he to be respectful of her, with some difficulty. The passion he felt for her was almost overwhelming. She was just as swept away as he was, but she didn't want to throw her heart over the wall too soon, and he didn't want to spoil the moment and the night by telling her he was married, even though it was to a woman he didn't love anymore, and who didn't love him. He and Matilda had become strangers to each other, and he had begun to think that their living arrangement had been a mistake. They should have ended it years before, but they hadn't, out of laziness, tradition, economy, and for a dozen other reasons that no longer seemed valid. But it was the path they had chosen a decade earlier, and the easiest one when they chose it by tacit agreement, and now he had to face the consequences of it with a woman he had met and knew he could come to care about. He owed her total honesty, and intended to give it to her, but he wanted to choose the right place and time to minimize the impact and any damages. When he drove away that night, back to town, after kissing her again, he promised himself he would tell her after the weekend.

He called her on Sunday, and asked her to dinner on Monday night, and she told him she was seeing her publisher, so she couldn't make it. He made a date with her for Tuesday night and promised himself he would tell her then. Then he realized that it was fortunate she'd been busy on Monday, since he had accepted a dinner engagement himself that night and had forgotten about it.

He dreaded Tuesday night, although he loved being with her. But he couldn't wait any longer, especially now that he'd kissed her. She deserved full disclosure, and an explanation of the circumstances. He had some serious thinking to do now himself, about what he was doing and where he was going. His life was about to become complicated, but it didn't deter him. Sabrina seemed like a miracle in his life, and nothing was going to stop him.

He sent Sabrina a text on Sunday night. Tuesday seemed like an eternity to wait to see her again. And he sent her an enormous bouquet of red roses on Monday. Three dozen of them, filling her room with their fragrance. She was sorry she'd accepted Felicity's invitation for that night, but it was going to be fun meeting people on the London literary scene too. She was sorry she couldn't take Gray with her. She was sure he'd enjoy it, but they each had their own lives to pursue. This was only the beginning.

She went shopping that afternoon and bought a simple red dress to wear to the party that night. She felt suddenly very brave and confident. She felt sexy and young and happy. She and Gray had a secret which no one knew. Just knowing that was empowering.

Chapter 6

Sabrina dressed carefully on Monday night for Felicity Parker-Smythe's party. She was interested in meeting the guest of honor, and liked Felicity, and was sure that the guests would be an interesting group, carefully selected from the literary world. Eighty guests for dinner was a big party. Sabrina did her hair in a loose knot and put on the new red dress, and black suede high-heeled pumps. The short dress looked great on her and showed off her figure and her legs. She'd been planning to wear the one "little black dress" she'd brought in case she got invited somewhere by her publisher. But the red dress suited her better. She was in high spirits. Meeting Gray and inheriting the Brooks estate were two very exciting events in her life, and she was in the mood to celebrate, even if no one knew what she was celebrating. She knew, which was enough. She wondered what Lawrence Vance, the guest of honor, would be like. She was sure he'd be fascinating to talk to, despite his strong opinions. His last book had been at the top of the bestseller lists for months, and was breaking all records in nonfiction.

The concierge had hired a car and driver for her. He was waiting downstairs for her when she left the hotel at eight o'clock. She didn't want to be among the first to arrive, and she didn't have far to go. She could see a line of well-dressed people entering the house when she arrived, and she joined them. Felicity greeted her as soon as she walked in and promised to introduce her to the guest of honor in a few minutes. There was a crush of new arrivals at the door requiring Felicity's attention, and Sabrina walked to the bar, asked for a glass of champagne, and blended into the crowd, observing the other guests. She saw two other famous authors she recognized. No one had noticed her so far, and she didn't mind. It allowed her to watch the other guests without having to participate, which she enjoyed.

The house was elegant, and the art was impressive. Sabrina was having fun just looking around and was pleased with her new dress. She could see the guests arrive as she sipped her champagne, and she noticed a small woman arrive with short uncombed hair. She was wearing black pants and a denim jacket and looked out of place among guests in chic outfits and some very avant-garde clothes. She didn't seem to care, and she had a stern expression, but seemed to know many of the guests, and Felicity greeted her warmly. She looked like someone from the literary world to Sabrina. It was fun trying to guess who people were.

Sabrina was startled to see Gray walk in. He stopped as soon as he saw the woman with uncombed hair and spoke to her for several minutes. He seemed to know her well, and he hadn't noticed Sabrina yet. She was delighted to see him there. It would be fun to share the evening with him. She waited for him to finish his conversation with the woman in the denim jacket, but he didn't leave her. He continued talking to her, although neither of them seemed to be enjoying the conversation.

"What are you doing here?" Gray said to Matilda the moment he saw her when he walked through the door. He wasn't happy to see her. They occasionally attended social events together, but he never enjoyed it. He noticed that she was wearing a denim jacket and was dressed inappropriately.

"Felicity invited me. We're on the board of the Tate Modern together."

"I forgot you were on that board," Gray said quietly. They hadn't been invited as a couple, and it felt awkward being there together. "William invited me," he said. Matilda knew he was one of Gray's biggest clients, so it was obviously an

accident that they had both been invited, and there was
nothing startling about it for their hosts, since they were
married. But if Gray had known Matilda was going, he
wouldn't have accepted. They never checked in with each
other about their respective social engagements, and it was
rare that they ran into each other, since they moved in separate
worlds.

Gray wanted to walk away but didn't want to be rude to
Matilda, just as Felicity swooped down on them and greeted
them both. She laughed when she saw them together.

"Great minds think alike," she told them both. "I invited
Matilda and William just told me he invited you, Gray. Come,
let me introduce you to some of the guests." She took them
each by an arm, and before they could say anything, she
forged a path through the crowd, introduced them to a few
people, and found herself face-to-face with Sabrina, who was
watching the threesome advance toward her with interest
and some confusion. She had no idea who the woman was,
but she was happy to see Gray, and smiled as he stood in
front of her with a look of panic. Matilda looked from her
husband to Sabrina and could see instantly that something
was amiss. Felicity was too busy keeping an eye on all of her
guests to notice.

"Matilda and Gray Abbott," Felicity introduced them to
Sabrina. "Lady Sabrina Brooks." She introduced Sabrina to

them with her brand-new title, as Sabrina's face froze when she heard Matilda's name, not her own. "And now if you'll excuse me, my dears, William is waving to me. I hope there isn't a fire in the kitchen," she said, joking, and dashed off, leaving the threesome staring at each other. Matilda knew Gray well and could see instantly that he and Sabrina weren't strangers to each other, and she extricated herself from the group as soon as possible with a comment to her husband.

"I'll let you deal with this." He looked like he was about to faint, and so did Sabrina. As soon as Matilda left them, Sabrina lowered her voice so only he could hear her. The room was full of the guests by then and the noise level was high.

"You don't have a sister, so I assume that's your wife. Or is it your ex-wife?" she asked hopefully. It was his last chance for pardon or mercy if Matilda was his ex.

"Not my ex," he said in a strangled voice. "We've led separate lives for ten years. I should have told you sooner. I was going to tell you tomorrow. We're married in name only."

"Do you live in the same house?" Sabrina asked him with an icy look. He nodded. He wasn't going to lie to her now.

"She travels all the time. We never see each other. I didn't even know she was coming tonight, or I wouldn't have come." It made no difference to Sabrina.

"You lied to me," she said, furious and wounded all at

once. "What was that? Some kind of game to you? You flirt with women and don't tell them you're married?" Neither of them noticed that Matilda was watching them from the distance, and she could see the fury on Sabrina's face. She was deathly pale and anyone could see she was upset if they looked at her. She didn't care.

"I didn't lie to you. I didn't tell you the whole truth, and I should have, but I never told you I was single."

"You acted like it. You courted me. You kissed me, for chrissake. What was the point of all that?"

"The point was that I'm crazy about you. You've bewitched me," he said, as quietly as he could in the noisy crowd. They hadn't moved an inch from where they'd been standing when they were introduced. "I thought if I told you, it would scare you off."

"It should have. You're a liar, Gray Abbott, and a snake. And what did you think would happen when I found out? I'd forget it or wouldn't care? You live with her, and you want to date me and go to bed with me?"

"It's never mattered before. I haven't met anyone I cared about in the ten years we've been leading our own lives. Now it matters, and I have to figure it out. I was going to discuss it all with you tomorrow. I see now what a mistake I've made with this arrangement."

"Don't bother explaining it to me tomorrow. I get the

picture. I thought you were a decent guy. You're not. Sins of omission are just as bad as sins of commission. You were lying when you kissed me."

"I wasn't," he said, looking desperate. "I'm falling in love with you. I've never felt like this about anyone. I'll straighten things out. Just give me some time to deal with it."

"Tell that to someone else," Sabrina said, shaking with fury, hurt, and humiliation. He was the first man who had actually meant something to her in twenty years, and he was married, and a liar. She had thought he was the best man she'd ever met. "Don't call me again," she said to him harshly.

"Sabrina, please . . ." he said, reaching for her arm as she pulled away from him, pushed her way through the crowd, and disappeared. They still had to get through dinner. He tried finding her among the other guests and he couldn't. He saw Matilda at the edge of the crowd, in animated conversation with a group of artists. Ten minutes later, Felicity and the waiters shepherded the guests into the dining room for dinner, where there were eight tables of ten, and mercifully, Gray saw that he wasn't at Sabrina's table or Matilda's. Sabrina saw, with dismay, that she was seated next to the guest of honor at the head table, and she would have to make intelligent conversation all evening. She felt as though she was drowning. It was one of the worst nights of her life. She had to put a good face on it for her publisher's sake, who had been nice enough to invite her. The whole evening had become a nightmare.

She managed to stick it out, and agreed with everything Lawrence Vance had said. She left discreetly shortly after dessert was served. She went outside to find her car. Gray followed her to the street and by the time he got there, she was gone. He felt like a complete heel, and he knew how wrong he'd been not to tell her sooner, but he had been afraid of her reaction and now he knew he'd been right. He was doomed either way. The moment she knew the truth, she'd have been gone, and not telling her had been the worst choice of all. It made him look dishonest instead of just scared. He knew she would have been no happier if he'd told her the next day. He had let her think he was single. It was wrong, but he didn't want to lose her, and now he had anyway.

She texted him from the car on her way back to the hotel. "Sell the property."

He answered as soon as he could write the message. "I will not sell it because you're angry at me. That's not the right reason. You love it. You could be happy there. It belongs to you. Don't sell it. Please."

"Find a real estate agent or I will. I live in Massachusetts, and you're an asshole. Sell it."

"I'm sorry, I was wrong, and yes, I'm an asshole, but I love you." She didn't answer him. He sent four more texts after that begging her to see him. She answered none of them. He was a married man, whatever he claimed his "arrangement" was with his wife. It was the mantra for all cheaters. She felt like an idiot for falling for him. And she had fallen hard. She was sure of it now.

She was back at the hotel by then, and called the concierge to get her a rented car at eight o'clock the next morning. She wanted to see the property one last time.

Gray called her until two in the morning, on her cell and at the hotel. She turned off her phone and told the hotel to hold her calls. She had nothing more to say to him. He was married. It was over, before it had begun. Her heart ached thinking about it, and she was too upset to even cry. She had been through torture with her ex-husband, and she wasn't signing on now for torture of a different kind. He was married and living with his wife. It was all she needed to know.

When she turned her phone on in the morning, he had texted her sixteen times. "Please give me a chance. Let's work this out. I'm sorry . . ." She had only one answer for him.

"You lied to me. I hate liars."

She got into the car in the morning and made her way through London traffic to the highway.

Gray woke up at eight o'clock the next morning and saw her single response. Her cell phone was off, so he called her at the hotel, and they told him she was out. He felt as though he had been run over by a train. She was the most amazing woman he had ever met, and he had blown it completely, and he knew she wasn't wrong. He hadn't lied to her, but he hadn't told her the truth either, and he could have. He didn't want to lose her, but he had anyway. He felt like a fool, and now she was going to sell the property. He realized that whether or not she kept it was linked to him now, too much so. And she realized the same thing as she drove there. She wanted to try to see it objectively before she made a decision, whether keeping it made sense in her life or not, regardless of Gray Abbott. She couldn't make the decision based on him, and shouldn't have, even if he were single. It had to be about the house and property, not about him. Gray was a separate issue.

When she reached the estate, it all looked familiar now. The well-kept farms, the tree-lined roads, the manor when it came into view. The lake in the distance. The gardeners neatly tending the flowerbeds that were a rainbow of color, and others that were delicate pastels. There was a quiet order to it. It all made sense and fit together like a beautiful puzzle. It would make a beautiful home for someone, she was sure, but not for her. It wasn't her home or her history. Her own history had played out in Boston and LA and San Francisco and New York, and now in the Berkshires. The Brooks estate was her father's history, and her uncle's, and even Gray's to some extent, but not hers. They were entitled to love it, not her. They had grown up with it, and she hadn't, thanks to her father's broken heart and his inability to forgive his brother. She had begun to fall in love with the house and the property, but she didn't feel it was meant for her. It was elegant, and Rupert had taken good care of it during his tenure, and had passed it on to her, which was generous of him. But seeing it clearly now, she felt it was meant for someone else, not for her. She was an interloper here. She didn't feel like the rightful heir.

It was what she had come back to see that morning. She had gotten confused. Her blinding attraction to Gray had made her think for a minute that she belonged here. She had wanted it to be true, but it wasn't. The Brooks estate was meant for someone else. She didn't know who, but it wasn't her. It had been left to her by default because there was no one else to give it to, no other relative. The title of Lady was hers, no one could take that from her, but the estate Rupert had left her belonged to someone else. Just as Gray did. Whatever their "arrangement" or their understanding, and whether he liked it or not, he and Matilda were bound to each other until they stood up and declared otherwise, just as they had declared their vows so long ago. Gray had tried to slip out the back door, and you couldn't do it that way. You had to leave via the front door, the way you came in. What Gray had done was real and it wasn't right. He had tried to masquerade as single, and she had believed him. But he wasn't. He was married, which was entirely different. She was giving it all back now, Gray to his wife, and if she truly didn't want him, that was between them. He still belonged to Matilda, whether he liked it or not. If he wanted to be single, he had to tell Matilda, not pretend to Sabrina. Whatever he convinced Sabrina of, however he fooled her, did not make him single, it just made him a liar in her eyes, and lying was exactly what he'd done.

Looking around the property in the morning sunlight, she wasn't even angry anymore. She was just sad at how it had turned out. But better sooner than later.

The property Rupert had left her could not speak for itself. She was the responsible party here, and needed to decide whether she wanted to own it or not, and do it justice, and put it in the hands of its rightful owner, whoever that turned out to be. She would have to leave the sale of the property to Gray. She couldn't do it well from a distance. Gray would have to sell it for her. She was sure now. Her uncle's estate was not right for her. It was too big, too grand, and it belonged to others, not to her. She felt free to leave now. Her decision had been made.

*

When Gray woke up in the morning, he felt battered. He felt like one of those old rodeo riders who have been in the bullpens for too many years. His failure to be straightforward with Sabrina had hit him hard. He had failed to pay the full price of entry for the ride he wanted to take, and he had cheated them both. She was too real a person, too honest, and had too much integrity for him to give her less than that in return. She was a real person to the tips of her fingers, and he had given her less than she deserved. He realized that now, and that she had a right to be angry with him. His own delusions about how free he was, and wanted to be, weren't enough for her, nor a reality. He and Matilda had never faced the degree of deterioration of their marriage and he had dragged Sabrina into it with him.

Matilda had appeared in the kitchen when he was making himself a cup of tea. He looked hungover, and she was in good spirits. She gave him a wry look and poured herself a cup too.

"An American?" was the only snide comment she made about Sabrina, and he felt rage rise up in him, as much at himself as at her.

"She's ten times the human beings we are," he said to her harshly. "We've made a mess of everything. This is a sloppy way to live. We turn a blind eye and the other cheek at whatever the other one does." He was sure she knew most of the times he had cheated on her, and there had been more than a few. And she had committed her share of indiscretions too. "It's not a marriage anymore. It hasn't been for years."

"It works well enough," she said complacently.

"Does it? Really? For whom? Don't you want more than this? We're riding on bald tires with half an engine. We're making do with less than either of us deserves." What he felt for Sabrina was honest and pure and passionate. It was real, just as she was. What he had offered her was flawed. He had offered her a cheap imitation of what she deserved, and she knew it.

"It's late in the day for us to expect more than that," Matilda commented. She was willing to settle for the little he gave her, and she had done no better for him, out of pure laziness on both their parts. It was easier to limp along as they were than to shut it down, leave, and start fresh. That took far more courage than what they were doing. This was such a poor imitation of what a marriage should be. There was nothing noble about sticking with it when their relationship was as far gone as this. They had won the endurance contest by breaking all the rules. "You must be very much in love with her," Matilda said quietly, "to set such high standards for yourself now, and for me. This works, Gray, as well as it can."

"No, it doesn't. This is a pathetic excuse for a marriage.

And it's not about her, it's about us. We never even tried to fix it when we could have. We just ignored it when the ship started going down and instead of shoring it up, or fixing it, we've been sneaking on and off the boat for years. Nobody has ever asked better of us."

"Some have," Matilda said cryptically. "I never stayed with them. I wasn't interested in making a life with someone else."

"You weren't interested in making one with me either. We're better than that, or we used to be." Sabrina had made him face the truth of what they'd become.

"Do you want to try to make a go of it again?" she asked with a look of surprise.

"No, I don't," he said. "It's too late for me." He didn't have anything left for her. He had to be that honest at least. He didn't think she had anything left for him either. They had lost each other years ago, and he had no desire to find his way back, and he didn't believe she did either. She didn't want to lose face, but this was about so much more than that. It was about having a marriage that was solid and you could count on. They couldn't count on theirs or each other and they knew it. They were no longer even friends.

"The children would be shocked if we don't stay together." She always dragged them into it when it was convenient for her. Her trump card, for years.

"Really? I'd be very surprised if they were upset. We've

119

given them another year of our pretending we have a viable marriage, for their benefit. It won't matter to them. They're already long gone, thousands of miles away, leading their own lives. What we do wouldn't matter much to them."

"It matters to me," she said firmly.

"It should have mattered to both of us a long time ago, and it didn't. We made a mistake in the beginning. We haven't had a real marriage in years."

"That's how marriage works," she said cynically. "Look at our parents' generation. They all hated each other and stayed married. None of my friends' parents shared a bedroom by the time we were old enough to notice. Few people I know have a better marriage than we do now."

"That's sad. And it doesn't make it right. If others are living on poison, why should we?"

"Because we made a commitment a long time ago. And we stuck with it." But what they had wasn't "sticking with it" to him, with frequent affairs on both sides. With Sabrina, he had found a woman he truly wanted.

Sabrina's life was about courage, honesty, and not settling for less. He and Matilda had settled for less every single day, for years. It was the example they had showed their children. Fakery. Dishonesty. Lies. Indifference. Turning a blind eye. It was a hell of a role model for them to follow, and he hoped they wouldn't in future years.

He went to shower and dress for work then. He didn't try to reach Sabrina again. It was clear she wouldn't see him. She sent him another text at the end of the day, when she got back to the city. She sounded calmer, and she told him that she was definite about selling the estate. She said it was more responsibility than she wanted to take on, and it deserved an owner who would love it and use it fully. If he didn't wish to handle the sale for her, she would find another law firm to do so. He responded that he would handle it for her, although he regretted her decision. He said he would send her the papers to sign, authorizing him to handle the sale.

He called her the next day to ask her one last time to see him. He called her at the hotel, and they told him she had checked out.

She was on the plane back to Boston when he called. She was relieved to be going home. She had been gone a week. She had learned enough about her history and her father to satisfy her. It had explained a lot to her about who he was and why he had had so little to give her. Her only regret was having been vulnerable to Gray. She had been happy and content with her life before she met him, and she knew she would be happy again. She had believed the lies he told himself, and the lie he was living. All she wanted to do now was to get back to her peaceful world in the Berkshires. She didn't need more than that. In a single week, he had shaken the delicate balance it had taken her years to achieve, but she knew she would find it again once she got back to writing, which always grounded her. Her life in the Berkshires was an honest one, which was centered around her work. It was the only life she wanted. She had fallen for the fantasy Gray offered her, based on a powerful attraction and the love she'd never found and had hungered for all her life. What he had offered her wasn't real. Gray wasn't real. She was. She was happy to be going home to her dogs, her work, her barn, and her friends Olivia and Steve. The one person she knew she could always count on was herself. Gray had reminded her of that. Her happiness was up to her.

Chapter 7

Sabrina's flight landed in Boston on time, and she went through customs quickly, with only the new red dress from Harrods to declare. Its cost was below the acceptable limit, so she had nothing to pay. She took an Uber home from Boston. She hadn't texted Olivia to tell her she was coming home. She wanted some time to herself to digest and recover from what had happened, before she had to tell anyone or explain it. It was simple really. She had fallen for an incredibly handsome, dashing, charming man. The chemistry between them had been breathtaking. He had turned out to be a liar, mostly to himself. He had told himself so many lies over the years that he believed them. He wanted to believe he was free, but he wasn't, so he had lied to her with what he didn't tell her. And, to take full responsibility for her part in it, she had been naïve. She should have asked him the question flat out: "Are you married?" He might even have told her the truth then.

He wasn't a total derelict or a psychopath. He just lived in an altered zone of what marriage could become if you let it; a twisted, convoluted, distorted relationship where no one ever faced the truth about themselves. It was everything she didn't want and it had never been acceptable to her. As much as she knew she would miss him now, and she already did, she preferred her life alone. It was honest, even if she was lonely at times. She hadn't been lonely before she met him. She had fashioned a life that worked for her.

In one of her groups for abused women in California, after she left Tom and was trying to recover, they had said that it was essential to have an "equal partner" in a relationship. Not necessarily financially equal, or even the same age, but of equal integrity, with the same values and philosophies about life. Cheating on his marriage had become a way of life for Gray, no matter what arrangement he and his wife had made, tacitly or otherwise. She didn't want that kind of marriage. She preferred none at all. She would rather wake up next to Winnie and Piglet every morning than beside a man who was lying to his wife to be with her. It made him a thief, in her eyes, of everyone's trust. She could have said that he had stolen her heart, under false pretenses. But he hadn't. She had handed it to him willingly, with total faith that he was what he appeared to be. She had been the fool, more than he the criminal. He had done what he was used to doing with other women and had been doing for years, assuming it would be all right with her too, and it wasn't.

He said now in his texts that he'd been planning to tell her in the next few days, because he was uncomfortable about it with her, but she didn't know if that was true. It didn't matter now. He hadn't told her. The scene at the Parker-Smythes' party had been embarrassing, for him even more than for her. For her it had been painful, a dagger to her heart, but the wound was clean. She had nothing to reproach herself for except her innocence and stupidity, as she saw it now. It had only gone on for a week, not an eternity. What he'd done was hand her a dream, and then smash it to bits. It was a hope that what they had discovered and were sharing would become much more. No promises had been exchanged. It might never have worked anyway, but it all seemed so wonderful for a few days, and so exciting and hopeful. She couldn't remember ever being that sure she had found the pot of gold at the end of the rainbow. She thought she had won the prize, that there would be a future with him and that it would be a happy one. Not a tawdry compromise while he stayed married and they lived a lie together.

It gave her just a glimpse of how heartbroken her father

must have been when Caragh ran off with his brother and married him, and when his second wife, Sabrina's mother, ran off with someone else. They were women without honor, and somehow without a heart, with utter disregard for the people they injured. Sabrina herself had been part of the collateral damage when her mother ran away with another man. She had been left like a forgotten object, a discard. She didn't believe that Gray had been utterly heartless, and he would have had to tell her the truth eventually, or someone else would have, but he was willing to risk it, to forget his marital obligations and his wife for what felt better to him in the moment, disregarding entirely how Sabrina would feel when she found out. She couldn't afford to be with a man who cared so little about the consequences of his actions, and their effect on her. A man with no integrity.

It had taken a toll on her, even after only a week of believing him. She had choices now. She could close the door forever on the possibility of meeting a man who might in fact be worthwhile. It was what her father had done after Simone, and she couldn't blame him after having lived the same nightmare twice. She could decide that for herself now too, and vow never to trust any man again. Or she could leave the door to her heart open just enough to allow someone else to sneak through one day, and take the risk that he might hurt her, or finally be the right one.

She hadn't decided which option to choose yet, and it was tempting to close that door. She had already decided not to accept the inheritance she'd been left in England, in the form of the estate. It didn't feel like a safe place to her now. She had led a small, controlled life in a safe place for her for the past ten years. She trusted the people around her in her life in the Berkshires. She took no chances and no risks. An estate in England, and a bigger, broader life, would expose her to more people, in an environment she couldn't control. Gray had just proven that. So she was eliminating that from her life, and staying in her much smaller world, where she was less likely to meet more worldly people.

Gray had just shown her that she was ill-prepared for those big leagues, so she was refusing the property and staying where she knew she was safe and could trust people, in her barn with her dogs. He had convinced her in a week that that bigger world was not for her. He had robbed her of that dream. She'd already been wounded in her life and didn't want to risk it again. Giving up the property in England was like her father retreating to his cabin in Vermont. It had been all he felt he could handle, and she understood why now, with deep compassion for him. She felt sure he had died of a broken heart at fifty-one, when he contracted cancer. She didn't intend to do the same.

She was not going to let Gray Abbott take anything more

from her. He had violated her trust and scared her off from taking the property she'd been given, but she intended to live her life to the fullest where she was and felt comfortable. She was going to write her books, love her dogs, and see her friends. She could hardly wait to get home to them now. The dog sitter was the only one who knew she was on her way. The Uber car pulled into her driveway and Winnie came bounding out like a giant white mop, with Piglet running more circumspectly behind him, her fluffy white tail waving wildly, as Sabrina got out and kneeled down and hugged them. They ran circles around her, barking, and the sitter, a young local girl Sabrina knew was reliable, and grateful for the extra money, stood by, smiling. It was a demonstration of pure love. Sabrina carried her suitcase into the house and left it in her bedroom. She came back to pay Gretchen, whose parents were Austrian and ran a ski school in New Hampshire. She looked like Heidi. The dogs loved her.

"You came back sooner than I thought," the girl said, gratefully putting the wad of bills Sabrina handed her in her pocket. She had added some extra because she'd come back early and didn't want it to be a loss for Gretchen.

"I got everything done that I needed to do sooner than expected, so I came back."

"You should have gone somewhere else in Europe for a few days," Gretchen said, smiling. Winnie was standing between them, wagging his tail and panting, and Piglet had climbed into her favorite bed and turned her back on them. Having greeted Sabrina ecstatically, she could now enforce two or three days of punishment for Sabrina having left her at all. It was Piglet's usual reaction whenever Sabrina went somewhere without the dogs, which didn't happen often. In a few days, Piglet always forgave her. Winnie didn't have a retaliatory nature and couldn't hold a grudge. He was just happy she was home.

"I wanted to come home," Sabrina said to Gretchen. "I have work to do. I'd rather be here than anywhere else. Just as Dorothy said in *The Wizard of Oz*, 'There's no place like home.'" She had just learned that lesson again.

"Did everything go all right?" Gretchen was a sweet girl. Sabrina thought of the immediate answers; that she'd gotten her heart broken, been made a fool of, and given up the idea of owning a six-hundred-acre estate, all in the space of a week. The only thing left was the title she'd inherited as a viscountess, which seemed more like a joke in her real life.

"It went fine," Sabrina said, and Gretchen picked up her backpack full of jeans and T-shirts and got on her bicycle to ride into the village where she rented a room. She worked for the local vet, which was how Sabrina had found her. She waved as Gretchen rode down the driveway and got on the road to town, and then she went back into her cozy barn and walked into the kitchen to open her mail. There was nothing important or of interest. Anything important came to her by email now. Her agent had already written to her in London to tell her how much she liked the new book. As she always did, she said it was a sure hit. It was even more convoluted than the previous ones, and the twist at the end even more surprising. Sabrina had kept the readers guessing until the last page. Even Agnes had been fooled in the end.

Sabrina was going to write a new book that summer, but she was still working on the outline, and she wanted to recover from her trip. It had left tire tracks on her heart and she needed a little time to get over it. She knew she would in the end. She had recovered from worse after Tom. The secret was staying busy, and writing a lot, and she intended to do both. That always worked for her when faced with a disappointment, which Gray had been. First he raised her hopes and then he dashed them. It was the roller coaster of life. She'd been there before, and survived. There were no shortcuts in the recovery, she knew that too.

When she checked her emails, she found that she had one from Gray. It started out as a business letter about the estate. He said he would be sending her documents to sign shortly, relating to his permission to show the property for sale. After the first paragraph, he apologized again in the second one. He said he felt terrible about how badly he had handled things, that the feelings he had expressed had been entirely sincere, and that he was deeply sorry that she had become the victim of the issues he hadn't resolved in his own life. She had opened his eyes to how unacceptable his situation had become, for him or anyone he cared for. He said that she was the most remarkable woman he had ever met, and he deeply regretted hurting her. He still hoped to see her again after his issues were resolved. He very much regretted her decision to sell the estate, and feared that his own behavior had influenced her decision, and hoped she would reconsider rather than lose an important piece of her own ancestral history. He felt as guilty over that as he did about the rest. It was a nice letter, and she felt the same stirrings for him as she read it, but she wouldn't allow herself to think about it, or about him. She was definite about selling the estate. She didn't answer him. He had his own life to live, and she had hers. At least it had happened fast and ended quickly.

She went for a walk in the woods with the dogs, and Piglet deigned to come with them, glancing over her shoulder haughtily from time to time to make sure Sabrina knew she was in disgrace. Sabrina carried her on the way back, since Piglet tired much sooner than Winnie, who could lope along forever, barking at squirrels and birds. It felt good to be home, but she was surprised to find herself thinking about the estate in England. Although she had only been there a few times now, and only spent one night there, she missed it. She was sorry too that she hadn't had the chance to see Gray's father again and say goodbye. He was a lovely person.

She thought about the lake, and the woods, riding along the trails on one of Rupert's horses, and the secret rose garden with Caragh's grave. It still amazed her how much damage one person could do to the hearts of others. She thought of both her uncle and her father, who paid a high price for loving Caragh, whose own time on earth had been so brief. The wounds she'd inflicted had long outlived her; for twenty-five years in her father's case, and more than fifty in her uncle's. It was a long time to grieve an impulsive young girl. Sabrina was thinking about weaving parts of the story into her next book, in a more violent version of course. In her version one of the brothers would have killed her, and the other brother would kill him. She smiled as she thought of it. She loved the way she was able to twist real life into fiction and come up with some incredible stories.

She slept soundly once she was home, played with the dogs, did some repairs around the house, and made notes for the next book. She had another movie offer, but still no series, and she'd been home for nearly a week when she finally called Olivia. She felt better than she had when she returned. To the naked eye she looked fine, but there was still a gnawing ache deep in her heart. Gray was a hard man to forget, but she was working on it. The estate still crossed her mind several times a day. As he had said, it was a beautiful place. Her five acres in the Berkshires seemed tiny now compared to six hundred acres, but she felt she had no right to that property. She didn't need it. Her barn and the woods around it were the right scale for her and the scale of her life.

"When did you get back?" Olivia asked, thrilled to hear her and know that she was home. They hadn't spoken in ten days. "I've been trying to leave you alone, while you decided what to do with the estate and fell for the lawyer. I figured you'd send me a text when you were ready to talk. So how was it? Tell me everything. Are you madly in love?" The handsome attorney was an unexpected bonus. "Come to think of it, don't tell me anything. Do you have time for coffee?" Sabrina smiled. It was comforting just hearing her voice. It was home.

"For you, yes, always."

"I'll be there in five minutes," Olivia said, and arrived in six, with her mane of curly red hair. She threw her arms around Sabrina and hugged her, and they sat in the garden with mugs of coffee. "I've been dying of curiosity. Steve kept telling me not to bug you. I figured he might be right."

Most of the time, they spoke every day, but Sabrina was grateful that this time they hadn't. She had needed time to digest what had happened and make good decisions.

"So, are you moving to England?" Olivia asked her once they sat down in a cool, shaded spot in the garden. Winnie and Piglet were sound asleep in the kitchen and didn't bother to join them. They had stopped following Sabrina around, afraid she would disappear again on a trip. And Piglet was no longer mad at her. She had given it up after three days.

"No, I'm not moving to England," Sabrina said quietly. She knew Olivia was worried about it, but was generous enough to want Sabrina's happiness too. "Actually," Sabrina took a deep breath, "I decided to sell the estate. I fell in love with it for a minute. It's a beautiful place, rich with history and tradition. My uncle took good care of it. It shows all the signs of a three-century-old home and property that have been respected and loved."

"So why are you selling it?" Olivia looked puzzled.

"It's not meant for me," Sabrina said. "I don't want to live there. This is my home and I love it. The Brooks estate should be someone's main residence, or for at least six months a year. It's too much for me. I don't need it."

"It's not about need," Olivia said quietly. "You already own it. You're not buying it. Why can't you write there? You actually could live there six months a year. You're not tied to a job here. Could you afford to keep it?"

"It supports itself, and my uncle left a fund to maintain it," Sabrina said, and Olivia shook her head.

"You're not making sense. It won't cost you a penny, and it sounds like you love it. Why don't you try it for six months or a year and see how it works?"

"It's too much for me. Why should I have an estate in England? It's six hundred acres."

"So what? There must be people taking care of it now. Is it in terrible condition?"

"No, it's perfect."

"And no one's asking you to mow the lawn yourself. It sounds fabulous."

"What would I do with it?"

"Enjoy it. Sabrina, what else are you going to do here for the next fifty years that's so exciting? You've been handed an incredible opportunity, a real gift, that will cost you nothing, and might open all kinds of new doors for you. Why on earth would you turn that down? I'm sorry to say it, but you sound like how you described your father, shutting himself away in a cabin in Vermont. You already lead a reclusive life here. Don't cheat yourself of something that might turn out to be wonderful. Now that you've seen it and love it, why not give it a chance?"

"I feel safe here," Sabrina said quietly, and Olivia felt sad for her.

"You could be safe there too. Don't hide here. You could have fun in both worlds."

"I can't believe my father never went back, except now I know why, since my uncle married the love of my father's life. He never forgave him for it. They both mourned her for the rest of their lives. She sounds like a wild, impulsive girl. She broke my father's heart." And Olivia knew Sabrina's had been broken before too. It made her a better writer, but she still had the scars from her early life. It made her more sensitive and more caring, but more cautious too, as she was now about the estate she'd inherited.

"What about the lawyer, the gorgeous hunk who you told me about?" Olivia smiled when she asked. She'd been wondering about it for the past ten days.

"Ahhh yes . . . the gorgeous lawyer. He forgot to mention a little detail when we had dinner and visited the estate. Minor oversight. He's married. I found out when we went to the same dinner party given by my British publisher and I found myself nose-to-nose with him and his wife, and my publisher introduced us. The lawyer in question nearly had a stroke. And so did I."

"Oh, Sabrina, I'm sorry, how awful." Sabrina had been so excited about him, and so sure he was single. "That must have been so awkward."

"Yes, it was," Sabrina agreed, with a hurt look in her eyes.

"Are they happily married?" Olivia asked.

"He says they lead separate lives, and have an 'arrangement,' the mantra of all married men who cheat."

"It's very European," Olivia commented, and hesitated, and then added her own experience to it. "I had an affair with an Italian once, during a bad patch with Steve. He was married too. I never did it again, but it happened. Steve never knew." Sabrina was startled, she wouldn't have thought it of Olivia.

"Gray had ample opportunity to tell me, and he didn't. He said he was afraid of how I'd react."

"Did you see him after the dinner party?"

"No. I refused to. I went back to look at the property again, decided to sell it, and then left. He sent me a million texts and emails. There's nothing to say. He lied to me, or he let me think he was single. He says they've both had affairs, and they stayed together for the kids." Olivia could see that Sabrina was deeply hurt and disappointed. He was a married man, and he had lied, or was not forthcoming with her. "We got along brilliantly. He seemed perfect, but he's married. I don't need the pain of something like that." Olivia didn't disagree with her.

"Maybe he'd leave her," Olivia said, but they both knew that most married men didn't, and Sabrina wisely didn't want to deal with the grief of loving him if he stayed married. "You used to talk about how your father closed himself off and didn't live his life. Maybe this is your test of that. You're refusing a property that fell out of the sky. And how long has it been since you had a date, until the attorney?"

"Forever. And I don't date married men," Sabrina said firmly.

"Maybe you should see him and talk to him and hear what he has in mind. Was he apologetic?"

"Very. But so what? He still did it, and he's married. He shouldn't have kissed me."

"It seems too bad to sell the property because he kissed you," Olivia said rationally, and Sabrina laughed. "Why let him deprive you of a gift like that? He scared you off." Sabrina felt a little stupid about lumping the two issues together when Olivia said it. She had a way of getting to the heart of the matter. "Dump him if you want to, but that's some chunk of real estate you're tossing in the trash because he upset you."

"I just think it's too much for me."

"A big property and a married man? Yeah, maybe. But why not take it one at a time? Why not spend a month or a few months there? You might love it."

"I already do," Sabrina said pensively. "I don't know. I'll think about it. I already told him I'm selling. He thinks it's a mistake too. But it's such a big place," Sabrina said to Olivia with wide eyes. Olivia could see that she felt vulnerable and shaken by the revelation about Gray. It had made inheriting the property seem frightening and overwhelming too.

"You should talk to Steve about it before you make up your mind. And there's no better way to get a guy out of your head than to meet another one. I still want to introduce you to Steve's big new client. He's really a lovely man. He writes screenplays, so you have that in common. He's written a lot of movies, and his wife was a well-known actress. She died in a ski accident seven or eight months ago. He has no kids, and he leads a quiet life. And he has houses all over the place. Steve told him about you and he said he'd like to meet you."

"Is he the ninety-year-old?" Sabrina said skeptically.

"Don't be so mean. He's sixty-two. That's only fourteen years older, and he's in great shape. He's very athletic, and he loves dogs."

"You said before he was short. How short?" It was just girlfriend talk; Sabrina wasn't really interested. She was still too upset about Gray. He had seemed so perfect, for about two minutes, before it all fell apart.

"He's about five nine or ten. He's not a six five guy who

played pro football. He's really a lovely guy. He's from Savannah. His wife was English and they lived in London. He moved back to the States when she died. He's a big skier, so he moved here instead of New York, because it's close to all the good ski resorts. And he has a house in Aspen."

"Mmm . . . maybe," Sabrina said vaguely, with no enthusiasm. The sudden loss of Gray was still too fresh.

"I'm sorry," Olivia said again when she hugged Sabrina as she left. "But think about the property some more. You might regret it if you sell." It sounded like she would.

"It was part of my father's story, and my uncle's, not mine," Sabrina said with a determined look. Knowing what had happened with Gray made Olivia more determined than ever to introduce her to Caleb Clarke, the screenwriter. She had a good feeling about him, and she was sorry Sabrina had had a disappointment in England. Olivia was sad about it for her friend as she drove home. Sabrina had such a wounded look in her eyes. She was angry and sad and hurt and surprised all at once. Olivia remembered the feeling from her own dating misadventures when she was single, and it was awful. Things like that happened to everyone at some point. You just had to bounce back. She hoped Sabrina would soon. She'd recovered from worse things in the past.

*

When Sabrina put their mugs in the sink, she noticed that she had an email on the kitchen laptop. She went to look and saw that it was from Gray. He said the authorization papers were ready for her to sign, which would allow him to show the property on behalf of her. He wouldn't do it himself, but someone in his office would. He said that an attorney had to be present when she signed them.

She answered him quickly. "Just FedEx them to me. I'll handle it. Thanks, Sabrina." What more was there to say?

Gray looked miserable when he read the terse answer. He knew it was all he deserved. She was different from any woman he had ever met, and he blew it. He felt like a complete jerk, which seemed appropriate to him too. She had fallen for him, and he had ruined it, by hiding the truth from her. He knew he'd regret it for the rest of his life. And she knew she'd never forget him.

Chapter 8

Sabrina had just come in from a long walk in the hills with both dogs, with Piglet in a little front carrier, like a baby, when she saw a car she didn't recognize come up her driveway, and the doorbell rang a minute later. She was still wearing Piglet in the carrier when she answered the door. Winnie barked, pretending to be a guard dog. Piglet was, in fact, much braver than he was, but rarely barked. Sabrina answered the door and found herself looking at Gray Abbott. She was too shocked to speak for an instant, as they looked at each other. Her heart gave a leap and she was half angry and half thrilled to see him, and didn't want to be either one. He was carrying a briefcase, and wearing jeans and a blazer.

"Who's that?" he said, pointing at Piglet still in the carrier on her chest, her tiny legs dangling as the Chihuahua stared at him and Winnie continued barking while frantically wagging his tail.

"That's Piglet," Sabrina said, as she took the Chihuahua out of the carrier, set her down gently on the floor, and stood up to face Gray again. He looked breathtakingly handsome, as always. Sabrina was wearing pink shorts, a T-shirt, and pink running shoes from her walk, with her hair on top of her head with a clip, and no makeup. Her body was flawless and she looked half her age, thirty at most. Together, they made a striking pair. "What are you doing here?" she asked, as they stood in the doorway.

"I brought you the papers to sign," he said, looking sheepish. "It was faster than FedEx." She smiled in spite of herself, and took a step back so he could come in. He followed her into the kitchen, and she offered him something to drink. All he wanted was water, and he didn't waste any time when she invited him to sit down at the kitchen table. He apologized again, in person this time, for not making full disclosure and behaving badly. He said again that he was intending to tell her, but he had waited too long to do so. He didn't expect to fall for her. Everything about her had been unexpected. She was just glad she hadn't slept with him, which would have made the discovery even worse, but she didn't say that to him. She just nodded and listened.

"You let me think you were single," she finally reminded him, and he looked deeply remorseful.

"I know. I'm really sorry. I actually thought I was, in all the ways that matter, like availability, but that's not the issue. You deserved to know that I had—have—a wife. I feel single. We haven't had a proper marriage for years. Our marriage died years ago for a thousand reasons. We stayed together for the kids, and after they left, it was just easier not to bother doing anything about it, which was lazy and sloppy of us. We've led separate lives for years. I never met anyone else I cared about until you. The people I've gone out with discreetly knew I was married. I never had a long-term relationship, so it wasn't an issue. I've just been coasting for years, and then I met you, and it was all different. You took me by surprise."

"Me too," she said in barely more than a whisper. She hadn't been alone in what she was feeling, which was nice to know, but that was even more reason to be honest with her.

"You knocked me off my feet. I never felt as close to anyone so quickly." She was so open and real and honest, as though she came from a different universe from the women he knew, who were artful or clever or cunning or smart or ambitious, but never real in the way she was, with no artifice or agenda.

"I think I fell in love with you the first day." She did too, but she didn't admit it to him. She was more guarded with him now.

"I was perfectly happy before I met you," she said. "I hate feeling like this." She felt broken, with a wound deep inside.

"So do I." He was dealing with guilt as well as loss. "I'm sorry to barge in on you like this. I had to speak to you at least once. I'm going back first thing in the morning. I'm staying at a hotel at the airport tonight. You wouldn't see me in London, so I came here." She was touched by it, and impressed, but not enough to alter her position about him, or her opinion. "I know I screwed up. I should have told you right away." He looked even more miserable than she did. "I like your barn, by the way. I can see why you love it here. It's so peaceful."

"It's a good place to write."

"Sabrina, at least keep the estate. Don't sell it because of me. Your uncle wanted you to have it. It belongs with you, and it would be a good place to write too." She listened, thinking.

"I live here."

"You can live in both places. Your work goes with you."

"I don't need a manor house and an estate in England." She was an unassuming woman. He already knew that about her.

"No one does. But you already own one. It's been in your family for centuries. Why not enjoy it?"

He took the papers out of his briefcase then and handed

them to her. They were marked with yellow tabs where she needed to sign them. He handed her a pen and she signed and gave them back to him. They authorized him and his colleagues to show the house for sale on her behalf. It was six-thirty by then, and she could see that he looked tired. It was eleven-thirty at night in London, and he'd been traveling all day, just so he could see her and apologize in person. The papers were a thin excuse.

She made him a sandwich then without asking him and set it down in front of him with a mug of coffee.

"You need to eat something so you don't fall asleep on the way back to the airport. What time is your flight tomorrow?" she asked in a flat, practical tone.

"Seven A.M. I have to check in at five for international. I'll get up at four, which is why I'm staying at the airport. It's fine. I'm still on British time." It was eight when he finished eating, after she signed the papers. He drank a cup of coffee, and he had a two-hour drive back to the airport with no traffic. She was afraid he'd fall asleep at the wheel.

"You can stay here in my guest room tonight if you want," she said in a low tone. He knew he should refuse but he was suddenly overcome by a wave of fatigue. He could barely keep his eyes open. He'd been so nervous about seeing her that he hadn't slept on the plane on the flight to Boston, and he relaxed once he was with her and he could finally talk to her. She had been avoiding him for days, and he doubted he'd ever see her again. He wanted to at least tell her how sorry he was, and how sincere he had been. He wasn't trying to take advantage of her or lie to her. He just got caught up in being with her, and in everything he felt. It was as though Matilda had ceased to exist. In many ways she had, a long time ago. It was hard for Sabrina to understand. He was so used to his own irregular status that it didn't seem to need explaining anymore, except to her it did. And he would have the day after the Parker-Smythes' party. Too late by then. The bomb had been dropped, and the damage done.

He thanked her for the invitation to stay in her guest room, although he didn't think he should. The barn looked cozy and relaxed and inviting. There were a few chic touches here and there, with some very handsome contemporary art. It was interesting to see her in her natural habitat. It was an easy place to feel comfortable in, with big swooping modern chandeliers, high ceilings in the main room, and cozy smaller rooms like the kitchen and her office. He stood up to leave and she could easily see how tired he was.

"You look exhausted," she said gently.

"I'm fine." She walked him to the door, and he hesitated, and couldn't hold back anymore. He knew it was the last time he'd see her, even if he sold the property for her. She wouldn't see him again. He gently reached out and put his arms around her, and kissed her for a last time, and the forces that had driven them since they met took over, and their bodies pressed together seamlessly as they clung to each other like drowning people. They had both been starved for affection for too long. They were insatiable as they kissed, and he pulled away for a minute to get air and clear his head. "I should go," he said in a raw voice, as all the torment he had felt for weeks ebbed away and desire took its place.

"Yes, you should," she agreed, while holding him so tightly he couldn't move, and she didn't want him to. "Why don't you sleep here for a few hours," she said, trying to be sensible. "If you leave here at three, you'll make the plane." He nodded and neither of them moved for a minute, and then finally she pulled away and led him to a comfortable guest room down a wide hall from her suite, with the walls covered in brightly colored art. It was a happy house and he could see why she loved it. He was trying to regain his self-control as he followed her down the hall and she led the way into the room where he could sleep. It was easy to see that he was too tired to drive. He was almost stumbling with fatigue.

She turned on the lights and they looked at each other from across the room. And without a word, the magnets deep within them that had brought them together in the first place pulled them across the room to each other with irresistible force until they flew into each other's arms and began pulling each other's clothes off in desperation. And this time she knew without question that he was married and that nothing between them was certain. They had no past and no future, only the present to bind them together with a bond so powerful they couldn't pull away from each other and didn't want to. They made love with all the passion of two people who had been starved for love for as long as they could remember, and when it was over, they sank into oblivion together, feeling as though their souls had been emptied, and their hearts filled, as they fell asleep in each other's arms.

Chapter 9

Sabrina woke Gray gently at two in the morning with a mug of coffee she set down on the night table next to him, and then she bent to kiss him, and he pulled her back into bed with him and held her.

"I'd ask you if that was a dream last night, but it was better than a dream. I love you, Sabrina. I'm sorry I made such a mess of this in the beginning. I don't think I've ever been in love before. I married what was supposedly the right girl according to my family and she turned out to be the wrong one very quickly. We were so young, and it never felt like a marriage to me. If love matters, I'm more married to you now than I ever was to her. She's not an emotional person. We're not even friends. I don't want to leave you. I'm terrified I won't see you again."

"Don't think about that now," she said softly, and kissed him, and he was instantly aroused. They forgot the time and made love again, and by the time they stopped, he was supposed to be at the airport. He looked at the clock on the night table and groaned.

"How am I ever going to leave you?" he said, their love-making still heavy in the air.

"Do you have to go today?" she asked him. "It's Saturday."

"I didn't think you'd want me around. Could I stay the weekend?" She nodded. She wanted him to stay as much as he wanted to, and they both knew the ground rules and the lay of the land now. There was no guesswork or pretense. They were two adults who loved each other, knew what they were doing, and wanted to be there. There would be no bad surprises this time.

"You can stay as long as you like," she said happily. She had missed him so much since she had left London, in spite of everything that had happened.

"I have court appearances on Tuesday, so I need to be in London on Monday to prepare with our litigators. I could leave late tomorrow night, if that works for you." He had never asked her if there was a man in her life, but he didn't think there was now. And when he asked her, she laughed.

"There have been a few very insignificant encounters in the last thirteen years, and none in a very long time. I put all my energy into my writing, and my love into my dogs. I had a traumatic marriage that ended thirteen years ago. I've been married twice. Once to a surfer when I was twenty-two, so he could get a green card, and four years later to a doctor who turned out to be a sociopath. I haven't had any serious relationships since then. And that's my entire romantic history." The information wasn't lost on him, and she'd told him some of it before, although not in detail. That, coupled with an emotionally crippled, withdrawn father and a mother who had abandoned her as a child, showed that her life hadn't been rich with people who loved her, which made her all the more precious to him. He had had loving parents, and a distant wife, and hadn't been much of a husband himself. But he had at least gotten two nice children out of it. She didn't even have that. It made him want to protect her from all the dangers and heartbreaks in her life, and he had already been one of them. It explained the feeling he had about her fragility, and yet she was strong too. She was an odd combination of vulnerability and gentleness, strength and determination, kindness and compassion, with a high degree of honor and integrity. She would be a lot to live up to if they wound up together. The end of the story was a long way down the road. All they had was now.

He called the airline and changed his ticket for Sunday night. He booked a seat on the last flight. It left at midnight and landed at Heathrow at noon local time. He could be in his office by one, which worked for him. He had no luggage to check, and nothing to declare. He sent a text to advise his office. Sabrina wondered if he had to let Matilda know, if she would wonder where he'd been. Since it was out in the open now, she asked him, and he smiled at the question. "We haven't advised each other of things like that in years. She'd be shocked if I did. I think she left for Istanbul last week with friends, but I'm not sure. My daughter Pru usually knows where her mother is if I need to know. I don't."

It explained a little more to her about why he felt so free and unfettered. It didn't sound like a marriage to her either. But she hadn't had a normal one herself. She and Jason had been more like pals than lovers, and nothing like husband and wife. Tom hadn't let her out of a room without her accounting for her whereabouts. He had hidden video cameras and spy equipment in their apartment so he could observe her while he was out, and interrogated her when he got home to see if she told the truth. He never believed her anyway. She didn't waste the little time they had now talking about him. Her traumatic years with Tom didn't matter anymore, and hadn't in a long time. She was over him.

They went back to sleep after he changed his ticket, and woke up at nine on a brilliantly sunny morning, with warm weather and a gentle breeze. She took him on a long walk, and then they made breakfast together, as the dogs ran in and out of the house from the garden. Winnie shadowed Gray and kept shaking hands with him, hoping for a treat, and eventually collapsed on the couch, snoring, and Piglet observed him and brought him her favorite toy mouse. It looked well-worn and much loved.

"They're awfully cute," Gray admitted, as he snuck them bits of toast and Sabrina pretended not to notice. "We had hunting dogs when I was a boy. They were faithful and fun to play with, but yours are awfully sweet, more like children than dogs."

"They're my family. It sounds pathetic, but they're good company. They sleep in my bed," she confessed, and he laughed and raised an eyebrow.

"We'll put that on a negotiation list."

"It's nonnegotiable." She smiled at him and he kissed her and laughed. It was a problem they both hoped they might have one day.

"You drive a hard bargain," he commented, and then they cleared up the dishes and showered together. They almost made it out of the house, before they wound up in her bed this time and made love again.

She packed a picnic for them, and they drove to a nearby lake and lay on the sand and talked for a long time. He loved the area and could see why she was happy there. And she loved what she'd seen of the estate, and was familiar with London and liked it. But she lived here, and he was anchored by a major law career in London, and was married. It was hard to see how it could work, but they fit together like two pieces of a puzzle in every other way.

"No one in either of our families has ever divorced," he told her as they lay side by side on a blanket on the sand, and moved it under a tree when the sun got too hot. "We've never discussed it. We never really considered it an option. We just moved into this odd living arrangement, which seemed to solve the problem of incompatibility, but it bears no relation to anything like what I consider marriage, and there isn't much point to it. I'm not sure if she'd care if we got divorced or not, or had some sort of legal separation. What are your thoughts on the subject?" he asked her, curious as to what she would expect if they were able to move forward at some point. He was going to discuss it with Matilda when he went back, but he couldn't guess at her reaction. There was a broad range of possibilities.

"I don't want to share you with someone else," Sabrina said simply, "except your children of course, but not a wife. And I don't love the official title of 'mistress.' Other than that I have no set ideas on the subject. Would a divorce cost you a fortune?" she asked hesitantly. It was a big subject.

"Possibly. I don't have a big fortune. I make a very decent

salary in the partnership, and I have investments. We've been reasonable about what we spend. And she's not an extravagant woman. I don't know if she'd be vengeful or not. We've got quite a nice house, which doesn't make much sense now that the children are gone. It's too big, and she's never there. She's always traveling somewhere with friends. She has a very pleasant life." He spoke as though it was about a distant relative, or a sister, or an old friend, not a wife. "I don't think it would make much difference to the children. They're long gone now, and it's no secret that their mother and I don't get on. We've had separate bedrooms for years. I have no idea how my father would react. He's very modern about some things, and shockingly old-fashioned about others. The subject has never come up, because it was never an option we considered.

"I suppose the system is better here and more honest. You don't go sneaking around having affairs with people's wives. If it doesn't work, you end it, and pay whatever it costs. The men I know who've gotten divorced only did so in order to marry someone else, and that can make quite a mess. The new woman is usually half the wife's age and a great deal more attractive, with a brand-new set of breasts that her future husband paid for," he said, and she laughed. There was a serious cultural disconnect in how they looked at it. "Clearly the chap was cheating for some time if he's ready to marry someone else. I supposed it must be awkward for the new woman if she's a decent sort, and even harder if there are children involved. I'm glad we're past that stage. Divorce is much more part of the culture here."

"People cheat here too," she added. "Americans aren't saints, but they do divorce more readily than Europeans."

"Most upper-class people in England don't get divorced, they just work around it, as Matilda and I did for all these years. I suppose we'd have done that forever, if you hadn't come along and put a spell on me."

"Maybe you put a spell on me," she teased him, and she rolled over onto her stomach, propped herself up on her elbows, and looked at him. He certainly didn't have easy times ahead, and there was no saying how his wife would react. She hadn't looked thrilled to see Sabrina at the Parker-Smythe party once she figured out that she and Gray knew each other, and Sabrina had looked like a threat in the sexy red dress and high heels. Matilda was reasonably attractive, and only a few years older than Sabrina, but she clearly made no effort and didn't care how she looked. She looked like a frumpy schoolteacher or an artist with her chopped-off, uncombed hair and no makeup. No one would have guessed they were a couple, although Sabrina assumed that Matilda must have been prettier in her early twenties when she and Gray married. She had just lost interest in her looks, she hadn't lost them completely.

"I don't want you to be my mistress either," he made clear to her as they lay on the blanket on the warm sand, "or for us to have to hide in the shadows. If I'm ever lucky enough to get free, you deserve a position of respect in my life. I would be incredibly proud to be with you, Sabrina. I want you to know that. And I won't settle for anything less for you."

"So would I. I'd be proud to be with you," she said, lying on her back again, as she gazed up at the leaves of the tree shading them, and he kissed her.

They ate their picnic lunch and swam in the lake. She drove him through two of the villages to give him a feeling for the area, and they stopped for a little while at a county fair, rode the carousel, and had popcorn, hot dogs, and ice cream. Then they drove to a mall with outlet stores so he could buy some shirts and underwear, since he had only planned to stay overnight. The mall was huge and fascinated him, and at the end of the afternoon they went back to the barn. She would have liked to introduce him to Olivia and Steve, but she wanted Gray to herself this time, with the limited time they had.

They had bought food on the way back and had corn on the cob and delicious fried chicken for dinner. She made a salad to go with it with lettuce and tomatoes from her garden. They made love again and watched a movie afterwards, a favorite of hers he had never seen and enjoyed until he fell asleep, and she kissed him and turned off the lights. She had set the dogs up in the kitchen with their favorite blankets, so she and Gray had full possession of her bed. They had packed a lot into one day. And they had one day left.

There was almost a wartime quality to the weekend they were spending together. They didn't know when they would see each other again, and under what conditions. Gray had made it clear when they talked that night that if he couldn't come to her offering a clean situation, they couldn't continue. He wouldn't do that to her. This wasn't a casual affair for him, and she was a woman he respected. So their fate rested in his wife's hands now, and how amenable she was to a drastic change and letting him go. She could make things very unpleasant and hold him hostage financially, given their long-term marriage.

It could be the first weekend they were spending together, or the last one, and there was no way to know which right now. It might be a unique moment in time never to be repeated. They felt, with every passing hour, as though they had always been together, and were totally at ease and perfectly suited to each other, but the fates might conspire against them, and it might be a memory to be cherished and never repeated. They wanted more time together, maybe even a lifetime if they were lucky, but there was no way of knowing if that would be possible, and he didn't want anything other than a respectable situation for her, and nor did she.

He worried about her if things didn't work out for them. What would happen to her? He could see how alone she was, particularly since she had no children. Her work was the driving force in her life and grounded her, but he felt she deserved more than that, although she didn't expect it.

He asked her the question and she hesitated before she answered.

"I've thought about it. If things don't work out, I'll probably love you forever. Even if there would be someone else in my life one day, he probably wouldn't measure up to you. But I don't want to mourn you. That would be too sad. I was happy before I met you, and I'd be terribly sad if things don't work out for us, but I want to be happy again. With my work, and my dogs, my friends, and my life. My father must have mourned Caragh all his life, when she left him for his brother, and probably after she died, when neither of them could have her. I don't want to turn you into a sad memory because you have a different life and aren't with me. My father had no life, he had no woman he loved, no friends; he never learned how to love me, or let me love him. That's not who I want to be. So, will I love you forever? Yes, probably, maybe. But I don't want to be sad over you, Gray.

"What we have now is fantastic, and we love each other.

I want to keep that memory as it is now. I don't want us to become a tragedy, or for your getting free from your marriage to ruin your life in some way. My work always saves me. As long as I have that, I'll be okay."

He wasn't as sure about himself, but he was impressed by what she said. "Happiness is a choice," she said, "except if something terrible goes wrong with one's health." But she had had ample opportunity to view her life as a tragedy, because of her parents, and Tom, and the good man she had never met since him who could be her partner, until Gray now, or because of the children she didn't have. She had a career that fulfilled her, good people around her who she had chosen carefully, a home she loved, and even her sweet dogs. She wanted to embrace what she did have, and to share it with him if he came back to her. But her happiness was her own responsibility. She wasn't counting on him to make her happy. Believing that had helped her survive the bad things that had happened to her. She wasn't a sad person and didn't want to be. It made him feel better about leaving her when he had to at the end of the weekend. It was good to know that she'd be all right and would strive to make it so. It also made it even more appealing to come back to her, and he didn't have to shoulder the responsibility of destroying her life, if he couldn't make it back to her for whatever reason. In a way, she had found the secret to a happy life, and the answer to how she had survived her childhood and any misfortunes after that. He admired her for it, and it made him love her all the more. She wasn't trying to make him responsible for future sadness. She was a survivor and a winner to the core, and no one had taught her that or served as a role model. It was who she was.

Gray took pictures of her on Sunday morning after breakfast, and of both of them with the timer on her camera. He wanted a set for each of them, so they could remember the sheer joy of the two days they had shared. It was a wish and a hope, and a promise of things to come if they were lucky, and something to remember tenderly on dark days, to remind them of how sweet life could be, and would be again one day.

They went to church together, which Gray said he never did anymore, and she didn't do often. But it was a bond and a silent vow between them, without saying it specifically. They lit candles together, which was a ritual she still loved from her childhood. She had gone to church on Sundays, although her father never went with her. He was a declared atheist, and she wondered now if Caragh had something to do with that too, or Simone, or both of them, but he never objected to what Sabrina wanted to do religiously. She had become less devout in college, when other pursuits caught her attention and took up her time. Gray said he played tennis on Saturdays, and golf on Sundays, usually with friends or clients. It gave structure to his weekends, which were solitary, but he liked going to church with her. They held hands during the service, made lunch at home, and went for another long walk afterwards. They left the dogs at home, so they didn't have to chase after Winnie or carry Piglet. He took pictures of them too. He wanted tangible souvenirs and memories of the weekend they had spent together. She was grateful that he had had the courage to come to see her, although she wouldn't have let him if he had asked her.

He asked about the sale of the estate again that afternoon, and if she was sure, and she said she was. He had seen her life here, and it was complete without her uncle's estate. She had loved seeing it, but she didn't need it. It was how she wanted to feel about him. She wanted to love him, but not need him for her well-being or happiness or survival. It was a hard goal to have, but she was determined to get there. Gray wasn't as sure he could. He wanted to be with her desperately, and couldn't imagine his life without her now. And he knew that if Matilda stood in his way and made it impossible, he would resent her forever, and probably never forgive her. Being forced to remain in a life with Matilda, now that he knew and loved Sabrina and wanted to be with her so badly, would be a living hell.

They spent the end of the day in bed, made love twice

with exquisite languor and tenderness, and she made him a light meal after he dressed. They had to leave at eight to allow for traffic, so he could check in at ten for his international flight, and she had offered to drive him so they could be together for longer. He left one of the shirts he had bought, a cheerful red check, as a souvenir of the weekend, and took the two others with him, and she tucked a pair of ballerina-pink lace underwear into his rolling bag, to find when he got home, since he assured her he unpacked his own bags. He was going straight from Heathrow to his office for his meeting at one o'clock, if his flight was on time.

He kissed her longingly before they left her house, and patted the dogs and gave them each a treat. Winnie barked as they left, and Piglet danced around them, wanting to go with them; they loved riding in the car, but Sabrina didn't take them.

She and Gray talked all the way to the airport, and she put her car in the garage. Logan was busy on a Sunday night. Businessmen were flying to other cities, and the international flights were full for the same reason. Gray had promised to let her know how things were progressing with Matilda. He had two trials coming up, so he'd be busy with work too. He'd let her know if he had any interested buyers for the estate. He secretly hoped there wouldn't be, and that he could talk her out of selling eventually, but she was definite now. It wasn't a snap decision, or a reaction to his not telling her he was married. She just felt complete with her life in the Berkshires and didn't want to take on more. Her writing devoured her time, and one home seemed like enough to her, and the one in the Berkshires was where she felt she belonged. She didn't want to move to England for him, and then discover that winning his freedom was impossible. It would lead her into exactly the shadow life she didn't want, and he didn't want for her, so he didn't insist, although he might later. They had to see how things went with Matilda once he talked to her.

Gray checked in for his flight and waited as long as he could to go through security. Then finally, he couldn't delay any longer. Thanks to his coming to see her, they had had this incredibly magical weekend, a moment in Paradise to remember forever, whatever came next. His tardiness in telling her his status had become irrelevant. Everything was, except the feelings they had for each other. The weekend had been a bubble, perfect in every way.

"Remember how much I love you; whatever happens, hang on to that," he said, and kissed her just before he entered the security area where she couldn't go without a ticket.

"I love you, Gray," she said simply. She stood straight and watched him go. He turned and smiled at her, touched his heart, and then waved and disappeared an instant later. She stood at the window until she knew his flight had taken off. He sent her a text with ten hearts on it. Then she drove home. She felt tears well up in her eyes and she wasn't sure if they were tears of sadness or joy. She had no idea where their story would go from here, and maybe she didn't need to know. They had this moment and had shared two extraordinary days. For now, it was enough. She couldn't ask for more. She had a book to write and a life to live now, and she had to live up to what she'd said. She wanted to make it the best life she could. She owed that to him, and herself, to honor how much they loved each other.

When she got home, Winnie and Piglet were waiting for her, and happy to sleep in her bed that night. Sabrina fell asleep thinking of Gray.

Chapter 10

Sabrina lay in bed the morning after Gray left, thinking about him. Winnie was tucked in behind her in his usual spot, and Piglet was snoring softly with her head on Sabrina's pillow. Gray's flight had arrived in London almost an hour early, due to favorable tailwinds. He had texted her when he landed, and she found the message when she woke up. He told her he loved her, and was going home to change, since he had time now before his meeting. When she woke up at nine that morning, it was two P.M. in London, and his meeting at the law firm was underway. He was back to his real life, and she had to deal with hers.

She had thought about something the night before, as she fell asleep. Learning about her father from Phillip Abbott had changed things for her. As a child, and in her teens, and later in college, she had always assumed that there was something seriously wrong with her since neither of her parents had ever loved her. Her mother abandoning her and her father never warming up to her had marked her deeply. Her assumption had been that she was not only unloved, but clearly unlovable. It had taken her years, and several shrinks, until sometime in her thirties she'd realized that there was something gravely flawed in both of them, and it had nothing to do with her. It had been a great liberation when she had finally understood that.

But what Phillip Abbott had told her about Caragh, and Rupert stealing her from his younger brother, had given her deep insights into her father and why he was so severely damaged. A loveless childhood, locked away in a boarding school for so many years—and that much she had known from her father—motherless at the age of twelve, whisked home for the trauma of his mother's funeral and sent away again the next day on a lonely train back to hell. The girl he loved deserting him in favor of his brother and dead three years later, and Sabrina's own mother repeating the pattern to reinforce his feelings of abandonment. Sabrina had "only" been abandoned once. Including his mother's death, her father had been abandoned three times by the key women in his life. It was no wonder he had never opened up to his daughter, for fear that she would abandon him too. Caragh was the missing link that explained everything to Sabrina. It didn't make her own childhood any better in retrospect, or her own suffering any more bearable, but at least it explained it to her. He was only half the equation. What Sabrina hungered for now was some insight into who her mother had been, what had driven her away, what suffering in her own life had caused her to reject her own child, and why she had left Sabrina's father. What had he done to deserve that? Perhaps it had been his fault. But in any case, at the age of six, it had surely not been Sabrina's. Sabrina was curious to know now who Simone was. Her earlier curiosity about her mother returned with a vengeance.

She realized too that if she was to love again, successfully this time, she needed to know more about her parents. They were the people who had formed and created her. However flawed they were, their subliminal messages would affect her for a lifetime. No matter what she discovered, she wanted to know about her mother. She had heard of people finding lost relatives on the internet, and she was eager to try it to locate her mother.

After feeding the dogs, she sat down at the laptop in the kitchen, looking for sites that located missing people. She found it to be surprisingly simple. When she had wanted to try to locate her mother in her early teens, her father had said that he had no idea if Simone had gone back to Europe, or where she might be in the States, or if she had married again and changed her name.

All Sabrina had to go on was her mother's maiden name, which she knew from her own birth certificate, Simone Angelique Vernier, and her mother's date of birth, which would make her seventy now. Sabrina also realized that she could have died young like her father and no longer be alive. She didn't know if that would be difficult or easy to find out. But she put in her mother's name, and within half an hour she had a Simon Vernier, a Simone Vernier, and a Simone A. Vernier who had the correct age and birthdate and lived in Coral Gables, Florida. There was a driver's license with a home address. In the photo on her license, which looked like a mug shot, the woman didn't look like the modeling pictures Sabrina remembered from the box of old memorabilia she'd found when her father died. But she had the same bright red lips Sabrina did remember so vividly. Her hair was white now. There was no phone number, but there was the address. Sabrina could write her a letter if she wanted to. She wondered if her mother would answer. It seemed unlikely since she had never corresponded with her before. All Sabrina could think of to do was go there and try to talk to her. It seemed like a bold plan, and her mother might not welcome the intrusion. But Sabrina was hungry for information, and she had a little spare time before she started her next book.

In a spirit of research and investigation, she called the airline and found that she could fly from Boston to Miami, rent a car there, and drive the short distance to Coral Gables. She could easily go there and back in a day, and when the ticket agent on the phone asked her when she wanted to fly, Sabrina surprised herself and blurted out, "Tomorrow." But she had nothing else to do, and it would keep her from missing Gray too much during the first days after their magical weekend. She had woken up aching for him that morning, and searching for her mother was a fascinating distraction.

She was excited about it all day. She spoke to Olivia but didn't tell her about it. The whole expedition might be a total bust and she preferred to tell her after, rather than before, if her mission was successful. She didn't tell Olivia either about Gray's weekend visit. She wanted to keep that private, just between them for now, which made it seem more special. She didn't want to trivialize it by turning it into girlish gossip. Olivia apologized for not calling her. She had taught a two-day art class at the county fair art show and had sold three paintings. So, she'd been busy too.

*

Danielle Steel

Sabrina drove to Logan Airport at seven o'clock the next morning, to give herself plenty of time to check in at nine for the ten o'clock flight to Miami. She had already reserved a rental car, which would be waiting for her at the Miami airport.

It was only once she was on the flight to Florida that she took full cognizance of what she was doing. She was reaching out to the woman who had rejected her forty-two years before and hadn't been heard from since. What if hearing from her daughter again was Simone's worst nightmare, something she had always dreaded, or what if a current spouse and possibly other children had no idea that she'd ever had a first child and a previous marriage? Anything was possible.

Sabrina got increasingly nervous on the flight and landed at one-thirty.

The rental car was waiting for her. It was a cumbersome blue Ford sedan that reeked of cigarettes, but Sabrina didn't care. She felt a little crazy pursuing her mother, but she had come this far, and she wanted to see it through.

With the help of the GPS, she reached Simone's address half an hour later. So far, it had been surprisingly simple. Sabrina parked outside the building and wondered what to do next. She didn't know where Simone worked or if she did; she might be retired at her age. And, if Sabrina waited for her to come home after work, she might not recognize her, and it would be a long wait. There was no activity in and out of the building at that hour, but there was a sign that said "Manager's Office," and advertised weekly and monthly rentals. The building looked seedy and poorly kept. The street had battered-looking homes lining the street, and the sidewalks were cracked in several places. Garbage cans were overflowing, and the neighborhood looked depressing. There must have been a better part of town, but this was where Simone Vernier lived.

Sabrina rang the doorbell of the manager's apartment, and a thin older woman in a flowered housedress opened the door a minute later. "We have no vacancies," she said to Sabrina, and was about to close the door when Sabrina handed her a twenty-dollar bill and blocked the door with her hand.

"I just wanted to ask if Simone Vernier still lives here," Sabrina asked politely, as the manager quickly pocketed the twenty.

"Yeah. Why? Is she in trouble? Are you a cop?"

"Not at all. I'm an old friend. I was hoping to see her. Do you know if she's working and what time she gets home?"

"You don't have to wait till then. She works at the dress shop around the corner. Julia's. She'll be there now. She's the manager."

"Thank you so much." Sabrina smiled broadly at her to reassure her. She wondered what kind of activities they had there that they worried about police. Maybe prostitution, or drugs. It made the building seem even more depressing. There was something tawdry about it.

Sabrina left the car where she'd parked it, and she could feel her heart beating as she walked around the corner. What if her mother rejected her again and told her to leave? Suddenly the whole idea of trying to find her seemed crazy. What difference did it make why she had left? She had, and there was no way she could fix it now. The wound had been too deep and it had taken years of therapy to soften the scar. Simone couldn't make up for that in a few minutes of conversation in a dress shop. But curiosity was part of the driving force now. Sabrina wanted to see what had become of her mother, to see the other woman her father had mourned till his dying day. She couldn't imagine that her mother leaving him had injured him as badly as Caragh had, but it certainly hadn't helped, and had deepened the earlier wound beyond repair.

She saw the dress shop as soon as she turned the corner. The façade was painted pink with a shiny black awning. The logo was a pink poodle, and the dresses on the mannequins in the window looked cheap. One of the dresses was all silver sequins, and another one was black with silver stars. They looked like the kind of dresses hookers wore. A bell jingled and Sabrina heard a chime when she opened the door of the shop and walked in. A tall, thin woman with white hair was standing near a desk, and a younger woman was behind the cash register. The two were chatting, and Sabrina could hear immediately that the older white-haired woman had a heavy French accent. It was an eerie feeling knowing that she was standing only inches away from her mother as she pretended to look around the store. Most of the merchandise was flashy, with sequins or metallics. Sabrina couldn't imagine that the shop did much business. She noticed that her mother was wearing a silver-sequined halter top with white jeans and high-heeled silver sandals. Simone still had a good figure, although her skin looked old and crepey in the halter top, but it was easy to imagine that she had been young and sexy nearly fifty years before when Alastair met her in Paris. But clearly, the attraction hadn't been reciprocal or long-lasting, given how the marriage ended.

"May I help you?" Simone asked Sabrina, who wanted to get out of earshot of the young girl. She pointed to a far corner of the shop and asked if Simone could give her some advice.

"Of course," the older woman said, and she followed Sabrina to a rack of cocktail dresses that were on sale.

"I wonder if you could help me find my size," Sabrina said

audibly, and then lowered her voice to nearly a whisper. "I'm so sorry to do this to you, but I didn't know how to reach you. I don't have your phone number. I'm Sabrina Brooks," she said simply. "I wanted to meet you. Would you want to see me somewhere later?" If she had pulled out a gun and shot her mother in the chest Simone wouldn't have looked more surprised.

"I prefer here," she answered immediately, and looked frightened.

"I come in peace. I just wanted to meet you, even once." Sabrina tried to reassure her, as Simone called out to the girl at the register.

"Tillie, can you go and get us some coffee?"

"Sure," Tillie said pleasantly, took a few dollars out of the register, and left a minute later. Simone looked tense as she studied her daughter.

"Why did you want to see me? We have nothing to say to each other. I left a very long time ago. You're a grown woman now. You don't need a mother." It made Sabrina wonder if Simone had expected her to find her sooner. Had she failed in her mission? But Simone definitely did not look pleased to see her now. There was no hug, no warm embrace, no tearful reunion. Sabrina wasn't sure what she had expected, but the woman standing in front of her had almost recoiled when Sabrina said she was her daughter, and she looked frightened and kept her distance. If Simone had regrets about leaving Sabrina as a child, they didn't show.

"I may not need a mother now, but I did when I was six. Why did you leave us?" It wasn't an accusation, it was a burning question that had gripped Sabrina's heart for forty-two years. She needed the answer.

Simone sighed before she responded, as though the story was too long to tell, but Sabrina had time and wasn't leaving.

"I married your father because I wanted to come to America. They paid us nothing in Paris then as models. I became a citizen when he married me. Boston was very cold, and I couldn't get work as a model there. And then I got pregnant. I didn't want a baby. I was a child myself. I was twenty-one. He made me keep it. But he was a sad man, always in his papers and his books. He never talked to me. We got married too quickly. I was too young to be married, and he was too sad. His brother married the girl he really loved. He still loved her when we married, and then he heard that she died, and he never recovered. He was even more sad. I wanted to have fun, not a baby. You cried all the time."

"That's why you left?" The reasons sounded pathetic to her. A depressed husband, a crying baby, not enough fun, and bad weather in Boston.

"No. I fell in love with someone else. He didn't want

179

another man's child. So, I left you with your father, and we moved away. I married him, and it didn't work. We got divorced too." So Sabrina and Simone had both been divorced twice. It seemed like the only thing they had in common. It wasn't much.

"Were you going to come back for me, after you got divorced?" Sabrina was looking for something that wasn't there. Simone looked puzzled by the question.

"Why would I go back to your father? I was unhappy with him. He was too English and I was too French."

"For me, maybe?" Simone shook her head.

"No, I'm not maternal." And Alistair hadn't been paternal. They were a perfect pair, a matched set. "I never wanted children." Neither had Sabrina. She wondered if it was some kind of curse, or hereditary maybe. "Do you have children?" Simone asked Sabrina.

"No, I don't. I never wanted any either, so I didn't have any." But Simone had, and just walked away from her mistake.

"I couldn't take care of you, and I didn't want to." What Simone said was so simple, honest, brutal, and direct that it took Sabrina's breath away. She had chosen her lover over her child, left, and never saw the child again. Sabrina didn't dare ask her if she'd ever missed her or had regrets. She could guess the answer from the way her mother looked at her. There was nothing there. She couldn't imagine two more different people than her parents. It pained her to even think it, but her mother looked cheap. Her father had always looked distinguished and aristocratic. He must have been desperate or drunk to marry her. Or maybe her sex appeal in her youth had seduced him. She wasn't ugly now, but she wasn't beautiful, and she looked her age.

"Are you happy?" Simone asked her.

"Most of the time." Sabrina was honest.

"Are you married?" Simone was curious about her too.

"No, divorced."

"I had nothing to give you," Simone said with a shrug. "I thought about you sometimes. I wondered what you look like. You look like your father." She seemed disappointed. She had left no legacy, no trace, not even her looks to the daughter she didn't want. She didn't seem happy with Sabrina's visit. She was a reminder of the distant past, a bad memory for her.

"I wanted to see you," Sabrina said softly.

"There's nothing to see. Age is not kind." It hadn't been to Simone. Her hardness showed on her face, her youth and beauty gone. She looked bitter and tired, used.

"I needed some answers. I have them now," Sabrina said. Simone nodded, and there was a long awkward moment as they looked at each other, an unbridgeable chasm between them, and nothing to build a bridge with.

Sabrina thanked her, and Simone didn't reach out to her. She kept her distance. All these years later, she still had nothing to give. She was an empty shell with no heart. Her beauty had dazzled Alastair in her youth, but that was long gone. She had been small consolation for the girl he had lost, which was why he had married her, Sabrina suspected now. To fill the void that Caragh left. It was the only reason she could imagine. He had Sabrina, but never the ability to connect with her. He had given up on life and retreated into his solitary world. It was a lesson to her. Her parents had wasted their lives and the gifts they'd been given.

What Sabrina understood even better now was how severely damaged both her parents were, and their inability to love at all. It was their flaw, not hers, and not her fault. She had been lovable, even if she hadn't been loved. It was the answer she'd been seeking all her life.

She walked to the door of the shop and looked back at her mother, who was standing there staring at her. Simone picked up a little red scarf and tied it around her neck and suddenly looked very French. It was hard to believe this woman was her mother. Sabrina took a last look at her, knowing she would never see her again.

As Sabrina left, the door closed softly behind her. She got

back in the car parked around the corner, feeling numb, and drove to the airport to fly back to Boston. She hadn't gotten the answer she hoped for, or even a hug, but seeing her mother had freed her. She had lost her mother at six, and she knew now that in reality she had never had one at all.

Chapter 11

When Gray's flight from Boston arrived at Heathrow in London ahead of schedule, he sent Sabrina a text, and decided to stop at home, drop off his bag, and change his clothes before he went to the office. He always felt filthy after traveling, and was happy to have the extra time to shower and put on a suit. He was old-school that way and preferred wearing suits and ties to work. Most of his clients seemed to prefer it too.

He was staring out the window, thinking of Sabrina and the weekend they had just shared. He didn't know why she had come into his life, but just knowing her had changed him. The compromises he had made in his personal life for so long no longer worked for him. Everything about Sabrina was so clear, nothing with her was obscure or ambiguous or duplicitous. She was a straightforward, honest woman. Being with her was like looking into a stream of clear water.

Nothing was hidden, and he understood even better now why she had been so upset when he didn't tell her right from the beginning that he was married.

Everything about his life with Matilda was the exact opposite. Nothing was ever clear, the waters were always muddy, they never said what they meant, or told each other the full truth, or confided in each other. They had been unfaithful to each other for years. He had been just as much at fault as she was, and accepted his part in the responsibility. Their relationship was no longer enough for him. He wasn't even sure why their marriage had failed. Everything was always swept under the rug and never discussed. Most of the time, he didn't even know who she was traveling with, when she'd be gone or when she'd be back. He suspected that Matilda had most of her affairs when she was out of the country with "friends." They rarely had names when she mentioned them, and supposedly weren't people he knew, although more than once he had discovered that she had slept with one of his friends. He had never confronted her about it. It just went under the rug with everything else already there. But it mattered. He guessed that her affairs had little meaning to her or her partners. Even the short time he had been with Sabrina had changed him. She set the bar high, and he preferred her standards to his own. He trusted her completely. She was trustworthy and she expected the same from him. She made him a better person and brought out the best in him. He loved who he was with her.

The weekend he had just spent with her was perfect. He loved her home, the little villages in the Berkshires, he loved being with her, the long walks they took, the nights of making love. He even loved her funny dogs and was grateful that she hadn't made him sleep with them, that she'd had them sleep in the kitchen while he was there. He had a great time with her. His life had new meaning, and now he had to deal with Matilda. He thought that she was traveling again. She had mentioned it the week before, but he hadn't paid attention to when, and he was startled when he saw her standing in the hall as soon as he walked into their home.

"You're here," he said, surprised.

"Where have you been?" she asked him.

"Boston," he said simply. He didn't lie to her, although he no longer felt he owed her the whole truth. The ground rules were about to change now.

"The American?" she asked with a raised eyebrow. It was her code name for Sabrina, and he didn't like it. It sounded dismissive and disrespectful. Sabrina was a lot more than just "an American." She was a brilliant, successful writer, and an extraordinary woman, and he loved her. He didn't answer Matilda's question.

"I thought you were going to Turkey," he said.

"It got canceled at the last minute. I'm going to stay at a friend's house in Lake Como next week."

"Will you be around this week?" he asked her. "We need to talk." She looked concerned when he said it. For the past week or so he had been different. She didn't know what it was or why, but something had changed. He was crisper and more precise with her, asked her more direct questions. Normally, he let things slide and never asked her anything. Now suddenly he was almost businesslike with her, and it worried her.

"I'll be here. What about tonight?" she asked him.

"I have meetings all afternoon, and I'll be too tired when I get home from work tonight. Maybe tomorrow." He didn't want to fob her off, but he didn't want to tackle difficult subjects when he wasn't at his best, and jetlagged.

He went to change then, as he didn't want to be late for his first meeting. He rolled his little traveling bag into his bathroom and opened it to find his shaving kit. He saw a wisp of pink peeking at him, pulled it out, and found the lace underwear Sabrina had slipped in the night before as a souvenir. He laughed out loud with delight when he saw it, and put it in the pocket of his suit when he left for the office. He wanted to keep her near him all day.

He looked impeccable as usual when he left for work. He arrived at the first meeting five minutes early. He had prepared most of the material he needed on Thursday and Friday before he left. Now he wanted his personal life to be as whistle-clean as his business life. He and Matilda had a lot of cleaning up to do. It was long overdue. They had to start by being honest with each other.

He had texted Sabrina from a cab to the office to thank her for the "souvenir." She texted back that there were lots more where that one came from, and to help himself any time. He was still smiling when he got to the meeting. He was visibly in a good mood. He and his team were well prepared and covered a lot of ground, and the meetings went well. He left the office at seven and was home by seven-thirty. He was planning to have a bite to eat from whatever was in the fridge, and then go to bed, watch some TV, and turn the lights off early. He was exhausted after a long day.

He and Matilda had had separate bedrooms for years, so no one was going to disturb him.

He was tired from the night flight and the meetings, and surprised to see Matilda in the kitchen when he got home. They rarely crossed paths at home. Now that both their children were living abroad, she was either out with her friends or traveling. He helped himself to some cold chicken, and she lingered in the kitchen. She was very cool and British, and had never been a warm, affectionate person. They'd had a similar upbringing and common friends and interests when they first married, which had carried them along, and then the children came. It was never a great love match.

"I know you want to talk tomorrow. Do you want to do it now?" she asked. He had already told her that morning that he didn't want to do it tonight.

"No, I don't. I'm exhausted. I flew last night, and I've been in meetings all afternoon. We can do it tomorrow or the next day. Not tonight." She could already tell that his tone was different with her. He was businesslike, and she could see that he was tired, but she didn't want to wait to find out what he had on his mind, so she pressed him about it, indifferent to how tired he was.

"I've been wanting to talk to you too," she said clearly.

"I told you, not tonight." He could hardly think straight, and he didn't want to start the ball rolling and get into unpleasant subjects so soon after spending time with Sabrina. He wanted to enjoy the afterglow of their time together. And he was so tired after the litigation meetings that he felt barely coherent.

"Do you want to give me a hint?" They were starting off

on the wrong foot. He wanted to be rested for their discussion. Her timing had never been great.

"No, I don't," he said bluntly. He wanted to eat, unwind, and sleep, in that order. Not broach a complicated, delicate, and potentially explosive subject with her. And he wanted to be at his best to persuade her to divorce.

"I don't see why we have to wait," she pushed him. "We're never home at the same time. We might as well take advantage of it now."

"You're awake. I'm not," he said, and tried to eat his dinner without losing his temper at her. She sat at the kitchen table, watching him eat expectantly, and he finally pushed his plate away. He couldn't escape her. "Fine. I don't want to get into a whole lengthy, serious discussion, but the way we've been living for the past ten years makes no sense. I think we have to deal with it. It's not good for either of us. We should have addressed it years ago."

"We've dealt with it the way everyone does," she said coolly. "Why is it different now?"

He decided to be honest with her. It was a new frontier for him. He took a deep breath. "I've met someone. Someone who could be important to me."

"The American," she said, visibly unimpressed. "I don't need to know the details. It's happened before." She dismissed it as an unimportant announcement, which annoyed him.

"She's not the issue. We are. We both deserve better than this, Matilda. It's not healthy, for either of us, living like this."

"This is what people like us do," she said matter-of-factly. There was no emotion whatsoever in her face or her voice or her words to him.

"We've done it for ten or twelve years now, that's enough. It's not good enough for either of us."

"I'm fine with it," she said, as though that was all that mattered. "Actually, it's odd that you should bring it up. I was going to suggest to you that I think we should make a go of it again. For the children's sake." It was a tack that had always worked with him before, but it wouldn't this time. It was clever of her to invoke the children, but even that no longer made sense. She liked the status of being married to him, the lifestyle and the freedom, and didn't want anything to change.

"They're not children anymore. And frankly, they don't give a damn what we do, as long as we don't do something shocking or embarrass them publicly. We're the only ones affected by this ridiculous arrangement we've wound up in. The children don't even live in England anymore. We do. I do. You're never here." There was no point of connection left between them, except their address. It had taken a dozen years to get here. Their marriage was dead, and she knew it too.

"I could slow down my travel schedule a bit, if it bothers you," she offered. It no longer mattered to him, and was convenient for him too.

"It's too late for that, Matilda. We've lived this charade for too long. We're not in love with each other. We haven't been for years. We live here like strangers, and not even friendly ones. I'm not willing to do this anymore." And he wanted to come to Sabrina with a clean situation, for both their sakes.

"That's why I thought we should make a go of it again. We always got along."

"No, we didn't. That's how we got here. And what? Start going out socially together again and pretend we're a happy couple? I'm tired of the pretense and I won't do it."

"Whatever it is you've gotten yourself into," she said coldly, "will end sooner or later. It always does. People from our background don't get divorced."

"They do now. And it's what I want. Not some sham that won't work anyway. I want a clean start."

"That's exactly what I'm suggesting." She sounded blithe about it.

"I mean with someone else." Everything she had said so far was completely unemotional and dismissed what he was saying to her. She was refusing to hear it. That was the trouble with their marriage. She had the warmth of a glacier.

"We have children together, we respect each other," she concluded.

"But we're not in love and haven't been for years." He didn't waver.

"We don't need to be in love," she said with a look of disdain. "It's not important."

"It's *very* important." Everything that she was saying was what was wrong with their marriage. And it was the exact opposite of what he wanted and had with Sabrina. Sabrina was exactly who and what he wanted. "We've had a good run, Matilda." They'd been married for twenty-nine years, and at least half of it, if not more, had been a phantom marriage. He hadn't wanted to tackle the subject with her that night, but their cards were on the table now, and her suggestion of "having another go at it" was exactly what he didn't want. They were both silent for a moment when the phone rang, and she went to answer it.

She asked a series of questions, and he couldn't tell what she was saying. Her parents were older, and her mother hadn't been well lately. She came back to the table and spoke to him matter-of-factly.

"That was Bridget, your father's housekeeper. He had a fall down the stairs tonight. He broke a hip, they took him to the hospital by ambulance, and he'll have surgery in the morning." She said it as though reading off a grocery list, and he stared at her, as he realized what she was saying. He stood up immediately and left the table.

"Did he hit his head?"

"She didn't say," she said unemotionally. "She only mentioned the hip."

"I'll go right away." Gray was too exhausted to drive for two hours, but he wanted to be with Phillip as soon as he could get there. His father was eighty-four years old, and people his age often deteriorated rapidly and died after a broken hip. He was panicked for his father.

He hurried up the stairs to his bedroom and was back five minutes later in jeans, a sweater, and a windbreaker. He had his car keys in his hand, and Matilda was still in the kitchen. She looked up when she saw him. Their earlier conversation was put aside, but not forgotten. It was only the opening round.

"I'm sorry about your father," she said coolly. Her attitude and tone of voice were no different than usual. She was completely disengaged. She didn't even seem bothered by his telling her he wanted a divorce. "Give him my best," she said, and went upstairs as Gray headed to the garage to get his Aston Martin. It was faster than the Range Rover, and he could dart in and out of traffic. It was just after nine by then, and he'd had a quick cup of coffee so he'd stay awake on the road.

He was in the car minutes later and headed into London traffic. It wasn't lost on him that she hadn't offered to go with him, and couldn't squeeze out a drop of emotion for him or his father. She had just demonstrated why he didn't want to be married to her anymore. She was the coldest woman he'd ever known. All he could think of now was his father. Gray had always been close to his parents, and it had been a hard blow when his mother died. He didn't want to lose his father now too. They had been wonderful parents. He felt guilty for not spending more time with his father since his mother's death. He knew how lonely his father was, but Gray was busy at work.

It took him half an hour to reach the motorway, and he concentrated on the road to stay awake and get there as quickly as he could. As he pressed the car toward the highest speed he could get away with, he wanted desperately to speak to Sabrina. He wanted to hear her steady, warm voice. He used his car phone to call her cell. It went to voicemail immediately. He called her again and had no idea where she was. It was five-thirty P.M. for her. He wondered if she was writing. She had been doing her research to locate her mother, and went out to buy groceries.

He didn't call again, concentrated on the road, and prayed that his father would survive. Sabrina saw both missed calls that evening but she thought it was too late to call him, and assumed he was asleep after his plane trip the night before. He hadn't left a message and she thought it was just a good-night call before he went to bed. She had no idea that something was wrong.

He felt like a child as he thought about his father's accident and what could happen as a result. He thought of his father's many acts of kindness to him, how understanding he had always been with Gray, even as a rambunctious teenager and the mischief he occasionally got into. Nothing dangerous, but annoying for a parent. He thought about how wise Phillip was, the good advice he'd given Gray for his career in the law. A thousand instances came to mind of all the times his father had been there for him and had never let him down. Gray realized again how hard it had been for his father when his wife had died, and how alone he was now, widowed, with Gray too busy to see him most of the time, or even call him, grandchildren who had moved away and only saw him at Christmas, and his best friend Rupert who had recently died. Phillip never complained or tried to make Gray feel guilty for the times he didn't see him because he was too tired to drive down from the city on a weekend, or just wasn't in the mood because it was raining or had had a long week. Gray remembered his recent tea with him and Sabrina and how kind Phillip had been to her. It was all racing through his mind as he pushed the Aston Martin to its limits, and finally reached the hospital at eleven-thirty and hurried inside to see him.

A clerk at the main desk directed him to the emergency room, where they were keeping him until the surgery the next day. Gray had called Bridget the housekeeper from the car for further details, but she had none. She apologized for leaving Phillip alone, but she was babysitting her grandchildren that night for her divorced daughter, and couldn't let her down, so she had left him at the hospital.

Gray walked the length of the hospital to get to the emergency room, down confusing corridors. They were busy when he got there. A nurse was with him, taking his pulse, as Gray walked into the cubicle. His father was asleep, or sedated. He wasn't sure which. He was a big man, taller even than Gray, and he suddenly looked old and shrunken, as though he had aged twenty years overnight. Without the vitality of his personality, he looked small and fragile and ancient, and as though he had slipped to ninety or a hundred since Gray had seen him only recently. He looked frail, and it terrified Gray to see him that way. It brought tears to his eyes as he whispered to the nurse.

"I'm his son. How is he?" He spoke to her in the hallway.

She smiled reassuringly at Gray. She was young and very pretty. "He's had something for the pain so he's sleeping. His vital signs are steady. They were worried about his heart when he came in. The shock mainly." Gray could hear a monitor beeping steadily, which was monitoring his father's heart, along with other functions. "He'll be better after the surgery tomorrow."

"When are they doing it?"

"At noon. The surgeon came to see him an hour ago. He approved him for the surgery." She left and said she'd be back in a few minutes, as Gray went back into the cubicle, pulled up a chair, sat down next to his father, and gently took the hand that didn't have an IV in it. Even his hand looked ancient and frail now, covered in spots and blue veins. Gray remembered how strong his father was when he was younger, and now he looked so old and sick and broken. His hair was standing up in wisps, and Gray smoothed it down. He gently kissed his father's hand, and couldn't remember his father ever being sick when he was a boy. Now he looked desperately ill. The first time Gray had seen his father cry was when Gray's mother died. He knew how much his father missed her. They had had a wonderful marriage, but even now Phillip didn't complain, and accepted her leaving him alone as part of the natural order of life, although Gray and his father both wished she had lived longer. She'd been eighty-two when she died, and had been frail for years before that, and had Parkinson's. His father had been infinitely patient with her and had nursed her until the end.

It was a long night sitting next to his father. Gray dozed

off a few times, exhausted himself. But he never left Phillip and held his hand all night. His father stirred a few times, and moaned, but didn't wake up, and Gray wasn't sure if that was a bad sign. He asked one of the nurses who came in and out frequently to check him. She explained that they were continuing to sedate him through his IV, and it was better for him to be pain-free and rest before the surgery. The pain and the trauma of the fall were taxing for his heart at his age.

Looking at Phillip in the shadowy room with the lights dimmed, Gray didn't see how he would survive the accident or the surgery. It felt like the beginning of the end to him. This was how it happened, and how people his father's age went steadily downhill and died in a short time, no matter how well they had seemed before that. Phillip didn't seem strong enough to recover, and more than once, Gray wiped away the tears rolling down his face as he watched his father and prayed that he'd survive. He wasn't ready to lose him. It dwarfed all else in importance: Sabrina, his miserable marriage to Matilda and the changes he wanted to make in his life, his own career, his children. All he cared about now was bringing his father back to health and extending his life for as long as possible. Gray wondered if he'd be bedridden now. It felt tragic as he sat there beside him. He was frightened, as waves of grief and panic washed over him.

Happiness

The surgeon came to check him again at seven in the morning. Phillip woke for a few minutes then and spoke to the surgeon. His voice was weak, and he seemed mildly confused, which the surgeon said was normal from the sedation. Phillip recognized Gray and asked him what he was doing there.

"I came to see you, Dad. You had a nasty fall." He had tripped over his cane, coming down the stairs. He'd been too impatient to wait for Bridget to help him, and had gone down alone, with disastrous results.

"I've had worse falls from my horse." But not recently, at eighty-four. "I tripped over my damn cane." He remembered that clearly. "You should go home; you're busy, don't waste your time sitting here with me." Phillip squinted as he looked at his son, as he wasn't wearing his glasses, and the doctor observed him. "Go home and get some rest, you look tired," Phillip said to Gray with concern.

"So do you," Gray said with a wintry smile. "I'm not leaving." Gray went out to the hallway to talk to the surgeon when he left. "How is he?" Gray asked him.

"A bit knocked up, as you can see. That's normal at his age. He's strong, and I think he'll do well in the surgery. We'll want to get him moving afterwards. That's where patients his age run into trouble. I'm hopeful he'll make a good recovery, although you can never predict what complications might occur. Let's hope he's lucky." Gray nodded and asked a few more details, and then the doctor left.

They would take Phillip to the operating theater at eleven-thirty, in four hours. Gray glanced at his watch after the doctor left. It was two-thirty in the morning in Massachusetts, and he didn't dare call Sabrina and disturb her at that hour. He was desperate to hear her voice and talk to her, but he had to wait. He went back into his father's room. A nurse was with him and he had gone back to sleep. Gray sat down in the chair next to him again, to continue his lonely vigil, with a flood of memories to keep him company while he prayed his father wouldn't die.

They came to get Phillip and put him on a gurney shortly before noon, only a few minutes late. The anesthesiologist had been to check him by then, and explained the details of the surgery to Gray. His own life had stopped; the only thing that mattered now was his father. He had told his office where he was, and his partners would cover for him for as long as necessary and attend his court appearances for him. They all had elderly parents by then, and understood. Matilda didn't call him but sent another text, sending Father Brooks her best. She seemed so emotionally incapable to Gray. It didn't surprise him, but it seemed so pathetic to him now. They had lived in a wasteland without mutual affection for so long. He didn't know how he could have let it go on for as long as it did. But he couldn't let himself think about her now.

Phillip was already drowsy when they put him on the gurney. His speech was slightly slurred. He wasn't wearing his glasses, and he needed a shave. He still looked very sick and slightly derelict as he gazed at his son.

"You should be at work. You don't have to be here with me. Go to your office. Give the children my love," he said, patting Gray's hand, and closed his eyes as they wheeled him away, and Gray stood there watching as they rolled him into the elevator and the doors closed. He felt as though he had just lost his last friend in the world.

It was seven o'clock in the morning in Massachusetts by then, and he tried to call Sabrina again. It was still early, but he was desperate to talk to her. It felt like centuries since he'd seen her instead of the time it had been. He had never needed to hear someone's voice more than hers right then, and he prayed she'd answer. By the time he called her, she was on a plane to Miami, and her phone was off. And he had no idea she had gone away. She hadn't spoken to him since she had located her mother after he left.

He finally reached her minutes after she got back from her trip to Miami, She had taken the next plane after she saw her mother. She could hear the anguish in Gray's voice.

"My father had a bad fall yesterday." He filled her in. "He broke his hip. I've been at the hospital with him, since last night." He sounded exhausted.

"Oh God, Gray, how awful. I'm sorry. Is he okay? Are you?"

"Better now that I'm talking to you. His housekeeper called at dinnertime after they took him in the ambulance. I got here as soon as I could. He had surgery today. They say he's doing well but he looks awful, Sabrina. He suddenly looks so old and sick." She could hear how devastated he was, and her heart went out to him. She would have offered to come, but didn't want to complicate things for him. She imagined that his wife was there with him.

She remembered how terrible her own father had looked at the end, riddled with cancer. Phillip Abbott was a healthy man, but he was very old, and a broken hip was dangerous at his age, and so was surgery. "What is the surgeon saying?"

"That he's in good health for his age, except for his arthritis, which is why he uses the cane. He fell going down the stairs without help. He's going to be a handful while he's recovering. I may stay with him for a while, and commute. But we're not there yet. I'm sorry to call you with all this." He felt better just hearing her voice.

"I'm sorry I'm not there with you," she said. She wished she could be.

"Me too." He didn't want to say it, but he felt like a child suddenly, terrified to lose the father he had always been so close to and admired and loved so much. She didn't want to ask, but she was sure his wife was with him, and she was touched that he had called her. Just talking to her was a comfort to him.

"I'm sorry I missed your calls last night and this morning. I went to Florida for the day. I just got back."

"Florida?" She hadn't mentioned it to him when he left. "A book signing?"

She took a deep breath. It was a lot to explain. "No, something strange happened after your father filled in a lot of the blanks for me about my father. History really does matter, and I've never known anything about my parents, except that my father was English and had walked away from his family, and that my mother was a French model. After knowing more about my father and my uncle, I had this overwhelming need to find my mother. I looked for her on the internet and found her. I was shocked at how easy it was. She's living in Florida. I found an address, no phone number. So I flew down to see her today. I had to get it out of my system once I knew where she was."

Gray was shocked by what Sabrina said to him. "How was that? It must have been very emotional after forty years."

"It was hard, and sad. I'm not sure emotional is the right

word, except maybe for how I felt. She's not a warm woman, and I guess I found out what I've always wondered. She had no regrets about leaving me. She was in love with someone else who didn't want me around. She describes herself as 'not maternal,' which is accurate. It was strange seeing her. She looks like she's had a hard life. She's divorced and lives in a seedy little building in Miami, in a poor neighborhood. She works in a dress shop, and she seems bitter about her life. I can't even imagine her with my father, although she was beautiful then, and he must have been running away from the memory of Caragh. She wasn't thrilled to see me. She was shocked. I didn't have the guts to ask, but I don't think she ever even missed me. And I would have been even easier to find than she was, if she'd wanted to. She must have seen my books around somewhere at some point. It put some things to rest for me. It's like I never had a mother at all. I always figured that she might have missed me, and maybe was too ashamed to reach out. She's not. She said she was curious about what I look like, but not much else. We never hugged or touched, and she was relieved when I left. It's like she's been dead for all these years, or was never my mother at all. She's a totally empty person. She has no other kids. She just walked away and never looked back." What she told him was so shocking that he was quiet for a minute, thinking of Sabrina and how she must have felt.

"I'm sorry, that's awful."

"It is, but at least now I know. I never had a mother, or a father really. There's no deep explanation for it in her case. She's just a totally hollow person, an empty shell. I don't know what made her that way, but it doesn't really matter. Somehow, I came out of all of it alive, and I'm not like either of my parents. She couldn't wait for me to leave when I found her. I only stayed in Miami for a few hours and came back."

Just as Gray had thought about her from the beginning, Sabrina was an extraordinary person. She had been through a nightmarish childhood and more than her share of trauma, and she was bigger because of it. She didn't use it as an excuse to hide, or not to feel or live her life fully. He and Matilda had no valid excuse, and they had been hiding from any kind of deep emotions for all these years. He was terrified to lose his father now, and worried about how complicated it would be to get out of his marriage, but after meeting Sabrina, he felt more alive than he had in years. Sabrina was a survivor in every sense of the word, and falling in love with her had made him brave and brought him back to life.

"So that's where I was today," she said. Surprisingly she didn't sound depressed about it, she sounded liberated and energized. "Keep me posted about your father. And what happened to your court appearances today?" she asked, concerned.

"My partners covered them for me. I'll let you know how he's doing, and thank you for listening about him. I didn't realize it would hit me this hard if something happened to him. I don't want to lose him. He and my mother have been the most important people in my life. I can't imagine my life now without him." He could be honest with her about how vulnerable he felt, because she had been equally so with him. There was no shame between them and no need to hide their frailties. They were safe with each other, and they knew it.

"I don't think you will lose him," she said. "He's a fighter and a survivor, he'll come through it. He survived losing your mom, and that must have been very hard for him too. He doesn't want to lose you either. He's very proud of you, Gray, it's written all over him." He had tears in his eyes when she said it. It was just what he needed to hear. He didn't tell her about the initial conversation with Matilda the night before and that she was resistant to the idea of a divorce. He and his wife still had a lot of ground to cover, and he wasn't going to let her refuse him, and had no intention of trying to revive their marriage. The only woman in the world he wanted to be with now was Sabrina, and he was going to find a way, whatever it took.

"I'll say a prayer for him," Sabrina said gently, and he promised to call her soon, and then they hung up. Talking to her had made a difference.

Happiness

In Massachusetts, Sabrina stood looking at her garden thinking about Gray and his father, hoping he'd survive. She had decisions of her own to make now. Her meeting with her mother had turned the dial again about how she viewed her own life, and what her goals were. She had a lot to think about, and much to decide.

Chapter 12

S abrina had lunch with Olivia at Olivia's house the day after her trip to Florida, and told her about meeting her mother. In its own way, the meeting had been powerful. Her mother's complete lack of emotion for her said more about her mother than about her. Just as knowing more about her father had liberated her, meeting her mother and talking to her had shown Sabrina that her mother's abandonment had nothing to do with her. She understood that now as an adult.

"It's crazy," she said to Olivia, over the salad they made in Olivia's kitchen. "I've talked about both my parents a thousand times in therapy without really understanding what motivated them, or why they didn't care about me. I had to be forty-eight years old and meet someone who knew my father and his history, and meet my mother myself, to understand who they were, and how completely incapable they were of human relationships, and to finally get that it had nothing to do with me or how inadequate or unlovable I was. It's sad for them, but incredibly liberating. They actually shortchanged themselves, more than they did me. I paid a price for it, but nothing compared to what they did. My father deprived himself of his home, his family, and every possible kind of human relationship, because of a girl he lost at twenty-six. He was incapable of relating to anyone else after that, probably including my mother. And she deprived herself of the only child she had and any joy I might have given her, and shirked all of her responsibilities for a guy it didn't work out with anyway. I think she was only about herself and no one else. What it teaches me is that I don't want to deprive myself because they were so hopelessly screwed up. I don't need to punish myself for what they didn't have to give."

"So where does that leave you now?" Olivia asked. She had deep respect for Sabrina's ability to analyze things and come up with the right answers and a positive outlook on life. Sabrina hesitated before she answered, but she had thought about it on the flight back from Florida.

"It might leave me in England, for part of the year at least," she said. "You said something like that when I called you from London. Why should I cheat myself of the amazing inheritance my uncle left me? My father lived like a hermit in a cabin, alone until the end. My mother seems like a bitter woman who missed out on my entire lifetime, and is alone now and doesn't seem to care. They made lousy choices. Why should I give up everything my uncle left me? I'm thinking that maybe I'll go to England, and spend six months there, living at the manor, and maybe dividing my time between here and there would be an interesting life for me. As you put it, what else do I have to do for the next fifty years? It's worth a try. If I hate it or it becomes a burden, I can sell it. But I think I want to give it a try first." Seeing her mother had freed her, Olivia smiled and was happy for her, but she was slightly suspicious of Sabrina's motives.

"And it has nothing to do with a certain married attorney, and wanting to be close to him, hoping that he'll eventually leave his wife?" She didn't want Sabrina to be pinning all her hopes on an impossible dream if that was what he turned out to be. Olivia had never thought that making major life decisions to win a man was a great idea. Sabrina had to make those decisions for herself, and Sabrina thought so too.

"Maybe a little. It would be nice to be nearby if he does manage to get free. He says he wants to, but I don't know how feasible that will be. If she wants everything he's got, he probably won't get divorced. Most men don't. But for the most part, I want to give it a try for myself. I own an incredible estate in England, thanks to some weird turn of fate and a blood relationship with people I never even met. Why not try it for a while and see if it suits me? I have nothing to lose by checking it out. If things pan out with Gray, it would be wonderful, but that's not the reason I want to go. I have to want it for me, because I think I deserve it, not because of him. I don't want to stalk him. I want to be with him if he gets free. If he doesn't, I may still love spending six months a year in England, and the rest here. It might open a lot of interesting new doors. I don't know why, but seeing the woman who gave birth to me liberated me. I can't even call her my mother. She isn't one, and never was."

"So when are you thinking of going over?" Olivia asked.

"Maybe in the fall. I want to write a book here this summer. I don't want to try writing in an unfamiliar place right away. I want to ease into it. I figure I'll stay here this summer, and then go to England in the fall." She looked excited about it, and Olivia was happy for her. It sounded like a sensible decision, to at least give the estate she had inherited a chance.

"Have you told Gray?" Olivia was curious.

"No. I wanted it to be my decision, not ours. And who

knows if he'll really get free and have the guts to see it through?" She hoped he would, but he hadn't even started that battle yet, and now his father was ill. "I may not tell him for a while."

Olivia had another thought then. "Since you're feeling so adventuresome and liberated," she teased her, "how about meeting Steve's client from Savannah? He's really a terrific guy. He spends time in LA and New York for work, and he spends most of his time in Aspen, but he and his wife fell in love with the Berkshires, so now he's remodeling a house here. He's an interesting man, and you're both writers. Steve and I really think you'd like him. I think he's lonely. His wife died seven months ago."

The last thing Sabrina wanted in her life was another depressed widower. She had dated several and found them morbidly depressing, and she was in love with Gray.

"Maybe later. It's probably too soon for him, and I want to get started on the new book. But thanks anyway."

She enjoyed spending time with Olivia, and she was excited about going to England in September. She was thinking about it when she stopped at the pet store in the village to buy dog food for Winnie and Piglet on the way home. She had had a text from Gray again, and he said his father was doing well after the surgery.

The owner of the pet store greeted her warmly, and they

were chatting when another customer came in with two enormous English bulldogs; a white female and a caramel-colored male. Their breathing was so loud they sounded like some kind of motor. The man with them was wearing a black T-shirt and black jeans, and he had snow-white hair and a well-trimmed white beard. He smiled at Sabrina and apologized for the noise. She couldn't resist talking to his dogs. The white female was named Blanche, and the male was Max. They were both friendly and excited to play with her, while their owner asked the storeowner for the supplies he needed. Sabrina asked him about the dogs, while they both waited for their orders to be filled. He said he had brought both bulldogs back from England, and asked her what kind of dogs she had. She noticed that he had a gentle voice, and a southern accent. He looked more like someone from LA to her. He had a sophisticated look to him, and he was wearing a wedding band, so he was obviously married.

"I have an Old English Sheepdog and a teacup Chihuahua," she answered his question, and they left the store at the same time. He was driving a Range Rover, and had to lift the dogs in. They had special seats in the back seat of his car. She smiled watching him. He was clearly another dog nut.

Gray called her as soon as she got home. He still sounded worried, but somewhat relieved.

"The surgeon said he did very well. He may be better off

than before after this. He's needed a new hip for a long time, but they didn't want to risk the surgery, because of his heart at his age. I'm staying at the hospital with him for the next few days." They talked for a few minutes, and he promised to call again soon with news. Matilda and his home situation had been put on the back burner for now. He sent his wife a text after he called Sabrina. All Matilda said in her response was "Glad to hear it." She was a woman of few words, with a very small heart.

Gray noticed the difference now that he had met Sabrina. She was caring and not afraid to express her feelings, and she was loving to him. Matilda lived behind walls of ice. He realized now how lonely he had been for so long. He had never faced it until then, and had just filled the void with other women occasionally, his work, and his children when they were younger. He had spent years compensating for what Matilda didn't give him. It seemed normal to him, but he realized now all that had been lacking.

She didn't come to visit his father, but dropped off some books at Gray's office for Phillip to read when he felt better. The gesture was thoughtful, but never warm. She was typical of a certain type of upper-class British woman of another generation, when emotions were rarely shown or expressed, and would have been interpreted as vulgarity or weakness if they were. Whenever she was away, and on foreign turf,

Matilda felt free to do whatever she wanted, let herself go, and have fun with no one to observe her. But with Gray, she was reserved and cold. And fortunately, she was warmer with their children than with him, although she wasn't effusive with them either. Her emotional capacity was limited at best.

Gray stayed at the hospital with his father for the first few days after the surgery, until he was considered out of danger, and then commuted to his office in London and slept at his father's home. He spent the evenings with Phillip at the hospital to keep him company.

Phillip was having intense physical therapy, was grateful for Gray's attention, and had regained his usual good spirits within a few days after the surgery. His stamina was proving to be remarkable. Gray shaved him every evening before he left, and was enjoying the time he was spending with his father. The accident had frightened Gray, and reminded him that due to his age, his father's time with him could be cut short unexpectedly at any time, which made every day more precious. He was relieved to have an excuse not to sleep at his own home in London. He still had to face his situation with Matilda, but his father's accident had given him a reprieve before the battle began. But he couldn't put it off forever. Sabrina was being very understanding and they spoke mostly about his father when he called her, and not his marriage.

Happiness

Phillip knew his only son well, and they were spending so much time together that he sensed that Gray was troubled about something more than his father's health. They'd been playing chess at the hospital when his father looked at him carefully. He knew that Gray was still staying at his home so he was nearby.

"Are you all right?" Phillip asked him cautiously. "Work problems?" Gray hesitated before he answered, not sure whether to open up or not, and then decided to seek his father's advice. Generally, he didn't like discussing personal matters with his father, and had a certain degree of male pride about not doing so.

"I met someone," Gray said in a voice so low it was barely audible, while appearing to assess the chessboard.

"It took you long enough," his father said calmly. "I wondered when that would happen, when you'd meet a woman you could actually care about." Gray was startled by his reaction and met his father's eyes. He saw years of wisdom there, and immense kindness. "Rupert's American niece?" he asked Gray in a gentle voice.

"How did you know?" Gray asked him, shocked.

"I knew it as soon as I saw you with her. Does Matilda know?"

"Only that there's someone, not who. She suspects it's Sabrina, but I haven't confirmed it to her. I don't think who is important. What matters is that our marriage has been dead for years, and we never buried it. We just moved around it like a rock in the stream and pretended it wasn't there. I want to deal with it now."

"Does Matilda want to deal with it?"

"Apparently not. She thinks we should give our marriage another try."

"That's only because she knows there's someone else. She's had ten or fifteen years to correct her course and get it right with you and she never has. Do *you* want to try again?" Phillip asked his son bluntly, and Gray shook his head, grateful to have someone to talk to, especially his father. Phillip's accident had brought them closer and made Gray even more aware of how much his father meant to him.

"No, I don't want to try again," Gray answered him honestly.

"Then don't," Phillip said, and Gray was surprised by his response.

"I told her it's too late, and she said that maybe for the children . . ." Gray looked hesitant. Matilda knew just what buttons to push, and always had.

"*Don't* live for your children," his father interrupted him sternly. "They have their own lives now, they're already gone. All of this," he pointed to his injured hip, "comes *very* quickly, faster than you can imagine. Don't waste the time you have.

Your mother and I loved each other till her dying day and even now. We couldn't have done it without that."

"That's not very English," Gray said, and his father laughed.

"Don't waste a minute, son. Life flies by. Take a chance, even if you get hurt and it doesn't work out in the end. You'll regret it later if you don't. Life is too long to spend it with the wrong person, a woman you don't love. Matilda is a decent girl, but you don't love her anymore. Your mother saw that years ago. The family was right, but the woman wasn't." Gray knew that was true too.

"I used to think the family mattered," Gray said. "I no longer do. I don't care about that now."

"There's nothing wrong with Sabrina's lineage, except maybe for the French mother," Phillip said, and the two men exchanged a smile. "Plenty of mistakes have been made among 'the right people.'"

"It's my fault too. We drifted apart, and I let it happen. It gave me the freedom to do what I wanted to. I should have faced it years ago. I chose to ignore her indiscretions so she'd do the same for me." Gray suspected that she'd had far more dalliances than he had. "It's liable to make a mess if we end it, and it will be expensive."

"It'll make a bigger mess if you stay," Phillip said, "and the children will get over it. They should have no say in the matter. They won't console you years from now if you give up a woman you love." Sabrina had changed everything. She wanted a clean slate and she deserved one. They all did.

His father was tired then. They put the chessboard away, and he dozed for a while, as Gray thought about what he'd said. He had been avoiding Matilda since the accident, and knew he had to face her. He couldn't put it off any longer and he had no intention of agreeing to her "try again" plan. It was over. He had a feeling she was going to punish him for that. She had a passive-aggressive side, never overt, but covert, subtle, and vengeful.

He called her from his father's home that night and made a date with her for Saturday afternoon. She hadn't come to visit her father-in-law, and she hadn't seen Gray since the night of his accident. Gray had heard his father's wise words, and he intended to follow them, whatever it cost him. And he had a feeling that Matilda would see to it that it cost him a lot.

Sabrina ran into the man with the bulldogs again when she went to the pet store to get eye drops for Piglet and shampoo for Winnie. He was buying new beds for his dogs, and looking at some leashes. He smiled when he saw Sabrina walk in. It was a warm day and she was wearing shorts and espadrilles and a T-shirt. The two bulldogs were trying out the beds, and Blanche's head was sticking out of a large red igloo.

"They're very particular about where they sleep," he commented to Sabrina, and she laughed.

"Mine are too. They sleep in my bed and take up most of it. They think it's their bed." She wondered if he was a summer renter, up from New York. He looked like it. He was wearing a black Rolex Daytona watch, and loafers without socks, with black jeans again. He was very attractive, and somewhere in his early sixties. They left the store at the same time, and they headed for their cars, with the beds he had bought. He stopped when she got to her car.

"Would you like to meet at the dog park sometime?" There was a fenced-in area in a park at the end of the village, where people took their dogs. She didn't usually go there, but many people did. "I'd love to meet your two. Blanche and Max don't have any friends here." It was like talking about children. He seemed pleasant, and he didn't look like an axe murderer. It was a friendly gesture. She didn't invite him to her house because she didn't know him. But the dog park seemed like a harmless suggestion.

"That would be fun," she said with a smile.

"Tomorrow? Five o'clock?" He looked hopeful.

"Sure."

She was writing the next day, but she took a break at five

o'clock and rounded up Winnie and Piglet, who were asleep in a patch of sun on her patio, cuddled up together. She put their harnesses and leashes on and got them in her car. She was wearing a pink man's shirt with rolled-up sleeves, denim shorts, and pink running shoes. She never dressed up when she was writing. The man was already there with Blanche and Max as Sabrina walked into the dog park and closed the gate behind her. There were only a few other dogs there. It was a weekday afternoon, so people were working. She wondered if her pet store friend was retired.

Winnie and Max took off running and playing immediately. Blanche sat down with a pained look, and Piglet approached her cautiously, while Blanche ignored her.

"She's lazy," her bearded owner explained. "She hates going to the park. She's a city dog."

"Piglet doesn't like going out either. She would sleep all day if I let her." He bent down to play with Piglet and she came to life for a minute, and then nudged Sabrina, wanting to be picked up. The man with the beard was smiling at Sabrina as she held the little dog.

"What would we do without them? I'm sorry, I'm Caleb Clarke." They hadn't introduced themselves yet.

"Sabrina Brooks," she said, petting Blanche, who looked like she was smiling at the attention. Caleb Clarke looked surprised.

"The writer?" She nodded. "I love your books. They're fantastically twisted. My wife loved them too." It was an odd statement, which could mean either that he no longer had the wife or that she no longer loved Sabrina's books. Sabrina didn't ask for an explanation. "I live in Aspen most of the time, I just moved here," he volunteered.

"I moved here from New York nine years ago. I love living here. It's a great place to write, and to live. It's so peaceful."

"I'm going back to Aspen for the summer in a few weeks, but I'll be back here in September," Caleb said.

"I'm going to England for a while then," she said, watching Max and Winnie chase each other at full speed, while Blanche and Piglet were content just to observe each other.

"I lived in London for ten years," Caleb said. "I moved back last winter." As he said it, Sabrina guessed who he was. He was the widowed screenwriter Steve was remodeling the house for, whom Olivia was so desperate to introduce her to. They had found each other on their own. "London is a great place to live. My wife was English. I wasn't sure how I'd like it at first, but it's a fantastic city. I was sorry to leave, but things changed . . . I lost my wife, and I decided I needed a change of scenery, so I came home for a while."

"I'm sorry about your wife," Sabrina said gently. He nodded and didn't comment. The fact that he was still wearing his wedding ring said a lot to her. He was still recovering, and mourning.

"I might have to go back in the fall myself, to work on a movie."

"Do you take Blanche and Max with you?"

"I probably won't this time. I'll only be there for a few weeks if I go. They're not great travelers. I'm going to leave them with my housekeeper in Aspen." Caleb and Sabrina were like parents in a playgroup, and he was easy to talk to. A cloud had crossed his eyes briefly when he mentioned his wife, and she felt sorry for him.

"We'll be staying in the country," Sabrina volunteered. "Winnie will love it. I'm not so sure about Piglet. She's definitely a house dog. Winnie tries to herd whatever he can. People, dogs, whatever he comes across." Caleb smiled.

"Are you working on a book now?"

"I just started one. I'm going to work on it here this summer, before I go to England. I love the summers here; warm weather and a little breeze." Max and Winnie joined them then. Winnie had leaves tangled in his coat, and both dogs were panting and worn out after a good run. They all left the dog park a little while later. It had been a nice interlude.

Caleb looked awkward for an instant when they got to their cars. "It was nice meeting you, Sabrina. Maybe we could have a drink sometime." She could tell that this was new to him and hard for him.

"That would be nice," she said.

"I'm renting a house for the year. I'm remodeling the house I bought." She didn't want to tell him that she knew his architect. She didn't want him to think they'd been gossiping about him. This had been a nicer way to meet than being forced together over dinner, despite Olivia and Steve's good intentions. Caleb didn't seem like he was ready for a whole meal with a stranger or a blind date. He still seemed fragile, from the way he spoke about his wife. She was still very much part of his conversation, even to a stranger. Sabrina respected that. She wasn't trying to pick up men at the pet store or looking for blind dates—on the contrary. He asked for her number, and she gave it to him, and he called her phone so she'd have his. "Let's do the dog park again some-time, if it doesn't interfere with your writing."

"That would be nice," she said, "or you can come to my place for a glass of wine. They can play in my garden." She told him where she lived, and his rented house was only about a mile from hers. They were almost neighbors. She thought she knew the house he had bought. It was a hand-some stone house that was a hundred years old and had been on the market for about two years because it was so expen-sive. It was a big house for a man alone, and Olivia had said he didn't have children. But he was a very successful screen-writer.

Winnie jumped into her car with his coat of leaves, and she strapped Piglet into a little seat she had for her in case the car stopped short or had an accident, and Caleb put the two bulldogs in their fancier seats, where they could admire the view. Sabrina waved as she drove away. It had been a pleasant break in her afternoon of writing. She was not surprised when he called her two days later, and she suggested he come to her place and bring the dogs to play in her garden. It was safe since it was fenced in and they couldn't wander off the property.

He sounded pleased to accept, and seemed more relaxed when he arrived, and brought her roses from the garden of the house he was renting, and she thanked him. She poured him a glass of wine and found some cheese crackers in the cupboard. He admired her barn and her art. He said a lot of things from his London house were still in storage and he was going to use them in his new house when it was finished. He was intrigued to hear that they had the same architect. He liked her house a lot. She knew it was much more informal than the house he had bought, but this was what she had wanted when Steve created the house from the remodeled barn.

She hadn't told Olivia yet that she had met Caleb. She

didn't want to get her excited. Sabrina saw Caleb more as a candidate for friendship. It was obvious to her that he hadn't gotten over his wife's death yet.

He talked about her while they drank wine in her garden. She had died in a skiing accident in the French Alps. Sabrina remembered reading about it now, since his late wife was a famous actress. She had hit her head, and had what they thought was a mild concussion, and she had died that night in her sleep.

"You never know what curves life is going to throw you," he said quietly. "We had a wonderful marriage. We both worked a lot, and we put off a lot of things for 'later.' And then suddenly something like that happens and there is no later. I was married to someone else when I met her. We'd been unhappy for years, and I pulled the plug on my marriage and married Jessica. We were married for sixteen years, and they were the best years of my life. I'm grateful we had them. Now I'm trying to figure out what to do with the rest of it. I don't want to just sit there looking back for the rest of my life, but I have to admit, it's taken me a while to start moving forward again. She was a happy person. She wouldn't have wanted me to mourn her forever, but she's a tough act to follow. I'm so glad I didn't cheat myself of the experience of being married to her. My divorce was a mess, but it was worth it." Sabrina thought of Gray when Caleb said it. "People talk about how short life is, which can be true. But it's long too, too long to spend it with the wrong person. My ex-wife is happy now too. She married a great guy who's much better for her than I was," he said, smiling. "What about you? Divorced, I assume."

"Yes. Two marriages. The first one was ridiculous, fresh out of college. I married a surfer buddy so he could get a green card." He laughed.

"That's about right for a first marriage. I married my first wife because we liked the same movies and the same rides at Disneyland. People shouldn't be allowed to get married in their twenties."

"You're dead right," she agreed. "I married my second husband when I was twenty-eight. He turned out to be a sociopath. I eventually escaped. I've been divorced for thirteen years, and I love it. I wake up next to an English sheepdog every day, and no one is trying to kill me. It works for me. My first three books were loosely based on my marriage. Now all the terrifying things I write are pure fiction."

"You always surprise me at the end of your books. I never see what's coming. I don't know how you do it."

"I love writing them." She beamed as she said it.

"I love reading them. The movies are never as good as your books. They scare the hell out of me," he said, laughing. And he looked at her carefully then. "I'm still getting back on my feet after Jessica. I'm not dating yet, but I've really enjoyed meeting you." He was warning her that he wasn't ready for romance yet, which was fine with her.

"Me too." She smiled at him. "And don't worry, I'm not shopping for a boyfriend or a husband. I'm happy with my dogs and my books."

"Not looking for romance either?" He was curious about her. She seemed very comfortable in her own skin, but she was a beautiful woman, and it seemed a shame if she was alone.

"Not really," she answered. "There's someone in England, who's trying to wend his way out of one of those bad marriages you mentioned. I don't know if he will or not. Being unhappily married can become a habit."

"It was for me the first time. I didn't even know how unhappy I was until I met Jessica. And as soon as I met her, I knew, and I headed straight for a lawyer. If your friend in England is smart, he'll figure it out pretty fast. If he doesn't, he's a fool." He smiled at her. He almost hoped he wouldn't. Caleb liked her, but his late wife was still a constant presence and he couldn't imagine being with another woman yet, and he had wanted to let Sabrina know, which seemed fair to her.

"I'll be fine whatever he does," she said quietly. "I'm excited about living in England for a while."

"Are you going because of him?" Caleb asked her. They were surprisingly open and at ease with each other.

"Not really. I inherited a house there out of the blue last month. From an uncle I'd never met."

"It sounds like there's a book in it," he teased her, and she laughed.

"I'm thinking about it. It's a three-hundred-year-old manor, and I could do some really scary stuff with it."

"I'm terrified already," he said, and got up to leave regretfully after two hours with her. She was easy to talk to and he enjoyed her company.

They had dinner together the following week at a local restaurant. It was a typical New England tavern and they had lobster for dinner. She still hadn't told Olivia that she'd met him, and didn't want to. It was blossoming into a friendship which suited them both. Olivia would have tried to push it into more than it was, more than either of them wanted or was ready for. Sabrina had Gray, or the hope of him, and Caleb still had the memories of Jessica, and had made it clear that he wasn't ready to move on. He didn't want to let go of his wife yet, which seemed reasonable to Sabrina. And maybe he never would. He was sixty-two years old and not looking to get married again.

Caleb was leaving for Aspen in a few weeks, and in the meantime, they enjoyed seeing each other for a random dinner or a glass of wine. She didn't usually see people socially when she was writing, but she could talk about the book with him, and she didn't need to make a fuss for him. Sometimes he just came over to let their dogs play for an hour. She could tell that he was lonely and still hibernating like a sleeping bear after the death of his wife. And she had Gray on her mind.

Chapter 13

When Gray went to meet Matilda for their appointment, while he was staying with his father, he
didn't know what to expect. They were used to being apart
for weeks at a time when she traveled. She sometimes went
away for a month, so there was nothing unusual about
that. Once Gray's father was released from the hospital,
Gray wanted to be there near him to make sure he didn't
fall again. And he didn't want a nurse. Phillip loved his
son's company. They talked about Gray's cases, and points
of the law. His father didn't interfere, but he made helpful
suggestions sometimes, and referred Gray to obscure
similar cases he could use in his arguments. He had helped
him several times.

Phillip came home in a wheelchair, to protect the new hip,

and the housekeeper helped him by day and Phillip at night. But the doctor wanted him to practice walking with a walker several times a day to help him get stronger and get steady on his feet again. And Gray was there to help him shower and dress in the morning before he left for work. He could hold him up in the shower and bought him a shower stool. Phillip was a big man but Gray was strong enough to keep him steady. He was shaving himself again. He detested being an invalid and treated like one, so Gray pushed him to speed up his recovery. The goal was to get him back on his feet, with the use of his cane again if he still needed it.

When Gray went to meet Matilda, she was wearing a new dress. It was a pink flowered print that looked like one of their daughter's, and not the sort of thing Matilda usually wore. She normally wore jeans and baggy sweaters, and comfortable clothes she could travel in, with safari jackets bulging with odds and ends in every pocket. She looked younger in the flowered dress, and she had made more effort with her hair, which was sticking up less than it did regularly. Gray never paid attention to what she wore. It didn't matter to him.

She was waiting for him in the kitchen, with a silver tea service set out, and proper linen napkins. He wasn't sure if her dress and the tea service were a good sign or a bad one, and he was meeting her with some trepidation. Neither of them had mentioned their marriage, and what to do, since his father's accident. Gray hadn't changed his mind about what he wanted. If anything, he was more determined after talking to his father about their marriage.

"How are you?" Gray asked her, after he let himself into the house.

"Fine," Matilda said stiffly. She was bored being stuck in London, and had postponed her trip to Lake Como to talk to him. "How much longer do you think you'll be staying with your father? The commute must be killing you."

"I'm getting used to it. I want to be there until he's solidly on his feet again. Bridget can't spend the night, she has to take care of her mother. And Dad doesn't want nurses."

"He can't expect you to play nursemaid forever," she said.

"I'm happy to do it for him. I'm grateful he made it through the surgery." Matilda wasn't as attentive to her own parents, and she had sisters to help her, which Gray didn't. He and his father had always been close. "He enjoyed the books you sent him." He didn't tell her that he thought she should have come to visit, and she should have thought of it on her own. He didn't want to push her. "So, where are we?" he said, as she poured him a cup of tea in the china her mother had given them for their wedding.

"I think we ought to give it another try and start going

out socially together again. I'm willing to travel less." She didn't look happy about it, and what she was talking about was appearances, not substance.

"That's not going to change anything, Matilda, and you know it. We've done all this before. We don't make each other happy. There's no point dragging it out. You'll wind up having another affair, to put it bluntly, and so will I. We probably never should have gotten married, but we did. We were young, and we have two wonderful children. Let's call it a day now, so we can both have good lives, alone or with other people. Our marriage has been dead for years. It's time to bury it and move on."

"And what am I supposed to do?" she said angrily. "Go on the internet for a new husband?"

"You haven't had any trouble finding other partners for the past ten years," he said tartly. "You'd meet better ones if you were single. This isn't about who we find next. It's about getting out of a marriage that has made us both miserable for years. We both know it, our children know it, half of London knows it. What you want to do is dress it up again and pretend it's still working. It isn't. You'll always be my family. We have children together, but we don't love each other anymore." It sounded harsh, but it was the truth and she knew it. "Pretending we're still married in any real way is lonely for both of us."

She didn't look crushed or disappointed or heartbroken. She looked furious. But as his father said, if being married to him was so important to her, she should have made more effort, and she hadn't. She didn't have a job or a career. She could have spent time being a better wife to him. She hadn't even been a particularly attentive mother. She had relied on the nannies to do everything and had been out with her friends much of the time. Once the children were in boarding school, she started traveling all the time. Gray hadn't even started having affairs until long after he knew she had, which had been humiliating for him at first, particularly when they were with friends of his. Now he no longer cared. She had been careless with their marriage, and with him, and he had allowed her to be. It had been easier to let her do what she wanted than to try to turn it around.

"Are you going to marry the American?" she asked him bluntly, with rage in her eyes.

"I have no idea. But I want to be free to date people openly, without sneaking around, or lying to you, them, or myself. When was the last time we slept with each other, Matilda? Seven, eight, ten years ago? I can't remember. Can you? That was your decision, not mine. I think you were in love with Anthony then, which I only figured out later because he told everyone he'd had an affair with you. That was embarrassing, to say the least. I wasn't keen on sleeping with you myself after that. You'd moved us into separate bedrooms by then, which was at least decent of you. I don't want to blame you for the past. I had my part in it too. I just want it to be over now. Surely you must want that too. You need to be free as much as I do."

"There's no one in my life right now," she said, and he almost felt sorry for her, but not enough to stay with her.

"There will be when you want there to be." She was fifty-one years old, but she looked older. She hadn't taken care of her appearance and hadn't cared in several years. She had traded on her youth, her name, her birth, and had made no effort on any front. It was all water under the bridge now. "Matilda, it's over. How do you want to handle it? I'd like to close this chapter of our lives as nicely as we can, respectfully."

"I want the house," she said, almost before the words were out of his mouth. The demand startled him.

"The whole house?"

"Yes."

"That's not reasonable or fair. The house is worth a great deal of money today." It was in one of the best neighborhoods in London, and he had paid for it in full. "Neither of us needs a house this size now. Why don't we sell it, and split what we get for it? It would be enough for you to get a smaller house or a nice apartment."

"I don't want a divorce, you do. So, I want the whole house. I'm comfortable here. Or maybe I'll sell it. I want support so I can travel as much as I want to, and I want the contents of the house, all the art and furniture. All of it."

"And what do I get? Nothing?" She could see anger in his eyes.

"You'll have your father's house when he dies."

"You're not being fair here."

"Why should I be? Or we can go on living as we do now. You can do what you want, and so can I, and it won't cost you any more than you're spending now." It was why many of his friends had stayed in bad marriages. Because it was too expensive to end them.

"I told you, I don't want to do that anymore. I think we're going to have to let our attorneys settle this, if we can't. I thought we could be equitable about it. Apparently not." He stood up then, and she looked at him with hatred in her eyes. Things were going to change, it was inevitable. He had made up his mind. But she had decided to make it ugly, and as expensive as possible for him, to punish him for wanting out, and for falling in love with Sabrina. He didn't know what the end of it all would look like. He had resigned himself to losing half of what he had, but not everything. "I'll be in touch," Gray said, and walked out of the house. He drove straight back to his father's place in the country, steaming over what Matilda was doing. They could both be decent about it and have an amicable settlement, but she was not going to let that happen. She was going to try to scare him out of it. But he wasn't going to allow it. He was not a fool.

He didn't say anything to his father when he got home, and he had calmed down somewhat. But he was disappointed that she wanted to be so greedy and unreasonable. They were playing dominoes after dinner when his father spoke quietly.

"So, Matilda wasn't agreeable today?" He could see it on Gray's face.

Gray played a double five and scored two points. "She wants everything," he said, trying not to sound as angry as he was.

"Don't give it to her," Phillip said, and scored three points. "You'll have to be strong. She's trying to scare you. You'll get to something sensible, and hopefully fair in the end." Phillip sounded perfectly calm, and Gray smiled at him.

"Thank you for the support."

"You're smart. You'll handle it. At least now you won't have any regrets, and you won't miss her," Phillip said, and Gray laughed. But Gray could also see that it was going to be a nasty battle, and God only knew how long it would take. He hoped Sabrina had the patience to wait. At least she'd be in England. He hoped he would have some kind of agreement worked out with Matilda by September. But it didn't look that way. They were off to a bad start.

Two days later, Gray was in a meeting with one of the partners when his secretary told him that his daughter was on the line and it was an emergency. He left the meeting and took the call immediately. It was dinnertime in Sydney, and Pru was crying hysterically.

"Dad, how could you?" she said, sobbing. He had asked Matilda not to say anything to the children until they came to some kind of civilized terms, and then they would gently tell them that they had come to an amicable parting of the ways. But clearly Matilda had jumped the gun, and Pru hadn't taken it well. He wondered what her mother had told her.

"Sweetheart, this has been coming for a long time. It can't be a surprise to you. Your mother and I haven't been happy in years. We'll both be happier this way, and we both love you and Stewart." He tried to calm her down and she just went on crying. So much for believing that the children wouldn't be surprised and would take it well.

"That's no excuse for what you're doing. You're insane!"

"Pru, people get divorced all the time. We're going to do this as nicely as possible, so everyone is okay with it."

"How can you say that to me? How dare you! And poor Mom." Gray had a strange feeling as he listened to her.

"What did your mother tell you?" Gray asked, suddenly suspicious.

"She said you're throwing her out of the house and you're not going to give her a penny of support. And you're marrying some American woman who looks like a tart and is after your money, and she's half your age, and she looks like a hooker." Gray closed his eyes as he felt rage boiling up in him like lava, and fought to keep his composure, for his daughter's sake. Matilda was a bigger snake than he had ever thought her capable of being.

"I want you to listen to me, because in future I'm not going to give you the details of my divorce agreement with your mother. But I want you to know the truth here. I am *not* throwing your mother anywhere. She is remaining in the house. I would like to give her half the value of the house if we sell it. Your mother wants the *whole* house, and it may come to that. She will have all the support she needs so that nothing changes in her life, and she knows that. I told her that clearly. I am *not* marrying anyone and have no plans to. There is in fact a woman I would like to date if your mother and I get divorced. She is *not* a hooker, she is a very successful writer, she is a viscountess, Lady Sabrina Brooks, and she is Lord Rupert's niece, and she's four years younger than I am. She's forty-eight years old and a totally respectable, decent woman. But I have no plans to marry her or anyone else. I'm sorry your mother upset you. I don't know what kind of game she's playing. But your mother will get a very generous settlement, she will not be homeless or without support. I have no intention of dating hookers, or women half my age. Now, I was in an important meeting. Calm down, and we'll talk about this whenever you like. You can reach me at Grampa's house any night to discuss it. I'm staying with him while he recovers from the surgery for his broken hip. I love you. And you can ask your mother why she told you a pack of lies like that. Now go and have a glass of wine and relax." He got off the phone a minute later and he wanted to kill Matilda. She had purposely gotten their daughter all wound up and tried to turn her against him. It was a hell of a way to tell their children they were getting divorced.

He walked back into the meeting a few minutes later, looking like he was going to kill someone.

"Problem?" his partner Andrew Barclay asked him, concerned, and Gray sat down with a sigh.

"Matilda and I are separating. It's long overdue. It's amazing how you think you know someone and you don't. Do you know a good divorce attorney?" Arthur looked at him with a sympathetic smile.

"Yes, the one I used. He'll cost you a bundle, but so will your ex-wife if you don't have a good attorney." He jotted down the name and phone number on a piece of paper and handed it to Gray. "Call him today. Before your wife gets up to any mischief. Is there another woman in the picture?" Gray nodded. "Then call him faster."

"Matilda is already up to mischief. She told our daughter that I'm marrying a twenty-five-year-old hooker. I have no plans to marry anyone at the moment."

"Good luck," Arthur Barclay said to him, and they went back to discussing their client's problem.

Gray called the divorce attorney after the meeting, and got an appointment for the following day, as a courtesy to Arthur, who'd been married three times, and was a pro at this, which was helpful. Gray felt like an innocent in a harsh new world.

Gray told his father about it that night. He had tried to call Matilda several times that afternoon and she didn't answer her phone. He sent her a blistering email instead about upsetting their daughter and lying to her.

"I'm not surprised," his father said to him when Gray told him about the call from Pru. "I've always thought Matilda had a nasty side to her. Hopefully, the attorney you're seeing tomorrow will have some good suggestions to keep her in check. Don't let this deter you. Wars are dirty, and if Matilda turns this into a war instead of a peace treaty, it will be dirty.

But you'll come through it." Phillip smiled at his son encouragingly. Gray hoped Sabrina would come through it too.

He called her from his bedroom that night and told her about the call from Pru, and what her mother had told her. He left out the part about Sabrina looking like a hooker. He focused more on the house and Matilda saying he wouldn't support her.

"This may get ugly for a while," he told her, sounding tired. It was late in England, and five hours earlier on the East Coast.

"I don't want you to do this for me," Sabrina said. "You have to get out of your marriage if it's what you want to do. But I don't want you to do it just to make me happy. I don't expect you to destroy your life for me."

"I should have done it years ago. I was foolish to hide my head in the sand for so long. But I thought she'd be more civilized about it. I didn't expect a war."

"There's a saying here that you don't know somebody until you divorce them."

"Apparently it's true. What's the point of lying to our daughter?"

"To turn her against you," Sabrina said quietly. She felt sorry for him. She was sure it was going to get even nastier, and expensive. She didn't want to destroy his life, but she didn't want to date a married man either.

"I'm seeing a divorce attorney tomorrow. He'll tell me what the ground rules are and what's reasonable. Maybe I'll just give her the house and have done with it." It was worth a fortune in the current real estate market, and she hadn't contributed a penny when he bought it.

"Listen to your lawyer. How's your father?"

"He's getting stronger every day. He's a hellion. He wants to start using his cane and give up the walker. I don't want him to fall again, but I think he's actually better than he was before the accident. I'm so lucky we didn't lose him. He has a strong constitution, and an even stronger will."

"And a wonderful son." She sounded so gentle and kind compared with the woman he was trying to divorce. All Matilda had done was strengthen his resolve to leave her, and he was less inclined to be generous with her if she was going to play dirty and manipulate their children. He hadn't heard from his son, Stewart, only Prunella. He didn't think Matilda would have the guts to play the same games with their son. Pru was younger and more gullible, and closer to her mother.

They talked for a little while, and Sabrina said the book was going well. She was just getting started with it. He was glad now that she was staying in Massachusetts for the summer. He didn't want her around if Matilda was attacking him and liable to do something crazy like embarrass Sabrina publicly. She was better off safely three thousand miles away in America. By September, when Sabrina was due to arrive, hopefully things would have calmed down and he and Matilda would have come to some agreement. In the meantime, for Gray, it was going to be a long, hot summer. He thought Sabrina was worth it.

Gray saw the divorce attorney the next day at lunchtime. His name was Matthew Higgins. He said that essentially, it was all going to be about money. When there were young children involved, they provided a heated battlefield rife with dissent and strong emotions. But Gray and Matilda were long past that point. With a twenty-nine-year marriage and his the only income, it was purely financial and about revenge if there was another woman. They discussed all the possible options and combinations that were acceptable to Gray. All of them sounded expensive and somewhat unfair to him. But there was no way around it if he wanted to get divorced. It was why so many men didn't. They preferred to live under the same roof with a woman they didn't like, and have a girlfriend or a mistress. It was exactly the scenario that he and Sabrina didn't want. He was going to pay a high price for it. Matthew Higgins wasn't cheap either, but Arthur said he was worth it, and Gray believed him. He left the office with no illusions about just how expensive it was going to be. Matilda and the attorneys were going to be the big winners. Sabrina had sent him an email reminding him that he didn't need to do this for her if it wasn't what he wanted. She didn't want to force him into a war he didn't want, or cause an inordinate loss of money. She felt bad that he was going through it, but it was the only way to come out clean at the other end, which was what Gray wanted now, whatever happened with Sabrina. She had woken him up to that.

After she sent her email, she wondered if he would actually go through with it. It was hard not seeing him. She wondered if he would have made serious progress by the time she got there. She'd just have to wait and see. Meanwhile, he had a four-hour commute every day, to help his recovering father. They were hard times for Gray at the moment.

She thought of what Caleb had said to her, that his divorce to marry his late wife Jessica had been the best thing he'd ever done, and it had been well worth it. She hoped that Gray would feel that way in the end and not resent her for it.

Gray had sounded discouraged that night, and overwhelmed. She was sorry not to be there to comfort him, but it was cleaner for her to be well away from his battles. The lawyer had told Gray that too. According to Gray's lawyer, the only way out was through it. She just hoped that Gray was equal to it. If not, she'd be on her own again. She was now, anyway. He was just a hope and an illusion for now.

Happiness

She realized that there was a chance that, faced with the harsh realities, and a huge loss of money, Gray would decide not to go through with it. It was his decision, and in his hands. He reminded her constantly that he loved her, and she believed him. She loved him too. And all she could do now was wait on the sidelines to see what happened. It was Gray's war to wage, not hers. And entirely up to him.

Chapter 14

S abrina had dinner with Caleb Clarke the night before he left for Aspen. She had enjoyed his company in the past few weeks, for a glass of wine at the end of the day, or a cup of coffee in the morning, or dinner. She hadn't mentioned him to Gray and didn't think she had to. They were only friends, although she really liked him. But he wasn't ready to let go of his wife yet, and said so openly to her, and she was waiting to see what Gray would do, and if he'd really swim free of his marriage, or turn back because it was too hard or too costly. There were times when she feared he'd back out of the divorce to save his money. But it would be hard to go back to Matilda now with a full-scale war on their hands.

*

Matilda got nastier day by day, and had hired the most aggressive female lawyer in London. She was careful not to accuse Gray of infidelity, because she was more vulnerable on that score, but she accused him of everything else, including emotional abuse, which was far from the truth, and demoralizing for Gray. She dragged the children into it at every opportunity. Stewart was avoiding both of his parents as a result, and Prunella was constantly manipulated by her mother and sided with her. It was a lonely summer for Gray. He was still staying with his father, commuting, and ended every day exhausted. There was no relief and Sabrina was three thousand miles away and seemed like a dream at times.

He wondered if he was fighting an imaginary war, and if Sabrina was real in his life. He hadn't seen her since their magical weekend in the Berkshires. She wasn't part of his daily life, and he couldn't see her or touch her. His lawyer told him it was just as well to keep her out of it, at a distance, and away from Matilda for now.

Sabrina was due in England after American Labor Day in early September. She wanted to have her book finished by then. She had a lot of packing up to do. Caleb had promised to visit her in September in London when he got there to work. He came to see her the morning he left, gave her a big hug, and told her to take care of herself.

"I'm going to miss you," he said, as he sat in her garden

with her for a last cup of coffee. Without making formal plans to do so, they had seen a lot of each other as friends, which seemed to work. She had finally admitted to Olivia that she'd met him and thought he was very nice, but he was still mourning his wife and not open to dating anyone, and Olivia was disappointed to hear it.

If he had been further down his path to recovery, and Sabrina hadn't met Gray, she would have been seriously interested in him, but the timing wasn't right for either of them, which seemed to be their destiny. Some relationships were like that. They looked as if they would have been perfect, but they never happened. What Sabrina and Caleb had instead was a warm friendship, which was the only thing possible for either of them right now.

"I'll call you from Aspen," he promised, as she walked him to the car. She was sorry to see him go. Their respective solitudes seemed to fit together comfortably. "And I'll see you in London." They both wondered if anything would have changed by then. Jessica hadn't even been gone a year, and that date was sacred to him. Gray was up to his neck in the divorce, and knowing he was doing it for her, she couldn't abandon him and didn't want to. But there was an element of unreality to it, having spent so little time together, their passionate romance having taken off like a rocket ship, based on very little contact before that, and none since. It was an isolated moment of time on which everything rested. At times she wondered if they even knew each other. It was hard to sustain an intense relationship from three thousand miles away without seeing each other.

When Caleb said goodbye to her, he held her in his arms for a minute and smiled at her. "Take care of yourself, my friend, and write a great book. I know you will." He kissed her cheek and drove away, and as he did, she realized that end-to-end, with all their brief spontaneous visits and meetings, she had spent more time with Caleb by now than she had with Gray. They met each other's needs for the moment. She was looking forward to seeing him in London.

Once Caleb was gone, she concentrated on her work, writing every day as she always did. She took no breaks except to sleep, but never for long, and ate haphazardly at her desk. The story grew in her head and on the computer, and the deeper she got into it, the less she communicated with the real world. She went days without speaking to Gray, and in the heat of battle with Matilda, and constantly stressed, he didn't want to complain to Sabrina and his emails to her got shorter and shorter. He never had anything upbeat to say and there was no good news yet. His days were one long negotiation now with Matilda. He felt like an accountant instead of a lawyer.

Happiness

It was all numbers and how far he would go. He pushed back occasionally, but most of the time he tried to find livable compromises, which she then wouldn't agree to. Sometimes he felt as though she was having fun with it, and doing whatever she could to torture him. It was all about money now, with no reality to it. He kept adding more money to the settlement and she always wanted more again. He reported the daily progress to his father, who was utterly disgusted by Matilda's greed and how badly she was behaving. But Gray had to see it through now, and finish what he'd started. Sometimes he was too upset and depressed to call Sabrina, and she felt guilty about what the divorce was costing him.

Caleb called Sabrina from Aspen, usually late at night, which was even later for her, but she worked late on her book. Sometimes he'd had a drink, on nights when he was the loneliest. He said it was agony being in the Aspen house without his wife. Everything reminded him of her, and her clothes were still in the closet and he couldn't bring himself to part with them. Sabrina finally got him to move them to a downstairs guest room, just so he didn't have to see them every day. She felt like his therapist at times, which was what he needed, someone to talk to, and she was willing to be that for him. He was still in a lot of pain. They FaceTimed sometimes, so they could see each other. Everything in her life was long-distance right now—she had a virtual friend and a virtual romance. Sometimes it made her feel crazy, as though she were on a planet where there were no real human beings, just images on a screen. She felt as unreal as they were. Her only live companions were Winnie and Piglet. Olivia knew not to bother her when she was writing.

Sabrina sat in her garden sometimes at two or three in the morning, when she took a break from her work and wondered what she was doing with her life. It was a crazy way to live. And then, like a vampire, she would go to bed as the sun came up, and she would sleep for a few hours and then go back to work on the book. Everything in her life seemed off schedule and upside down and out of kilter.

She felt as though she was hanging in space all summer as she worked on the book. She was waiting for news from Gray, but nothing seemed to change there. She heard from Caleb at weird hours, and he talked about Jessica and how much he missed her. Sabrina felt as though nothing in her life was moving. It was as though production assistants were running past her carrying the scenery to give her the impression that the bus was moving, but in fact, it was standing still and going nowhere.

The reports by text from Gray were the same every day. No agreement had been reached with Matilda, and Sabrina wondered if it ever would be. Gray started to get testy with

Sabrina, because he felt guilty that Matilda wouldn't agree to anything.

In August, Caleb started working on a new screenplay. He sounded better, spoke of Jessica a little less often, and stopped visiting her clothes in the guest room to smell her perfume, which was an improvement. He said that Sabrina was the only one getting him through it, and she was the only person he could talk to. It was a heavy weight at times.

She talked to Caleb about her writing. It was hard to talk to Gray now about anything. His nerves were on edge and everything upset him. She knew that if she told him about Caleb, he would panic and be jealous, but nothing had happened between them. It was all platonic, unlike her relationship with Gray, which was physical and passionate, but felt like a fantasy or an illusion. She hadn't seen him in two months and had only spent one weekend with him, and a few days in England before that, before she found out about his wife and stormed off. Now Gray was trying to clean it all up, offering Matilda vast amounts of money that were never enough.

Everything in Sabrina's life seemed surreal on all sides. And she was starting to lose hope that Gray would get out of his marriage.

It was the strangest summer of her life, which turned up in the book too.

She finally finished the book on the last day of August. Caleb congratulated her when she FaceTimed him in Aspen, and Gray stopped complaining about Matilda long enough to tell her he was proud of her. They hadn't spoken in a week because he hated telling her the same thing over and over, that Matilda had turned down another proposal. His final offer was on the table now, and he wasn't optimistic that she'd accept it. She hadn't accepted a single one of his offers in more than two months. He had begun to think that a divorce would be impossible, but he didn't want to tell Sabrina that, so he had been avoiding her until he had something positive to tell her. Both Gray and Caleb had begun to seem unreal in her life, but she felt better once she finished the book, with a wild flourish and a surprise ending more daring than anything she'd written before. Even Agnes was shocked when she read it after Sabrina emailed it to her.

"That ending is absolutely insane," Agnes said to her, and Sabrina was delighted. "I think you're certifiably crazy."

"I think so too. I've had a crazy summer." It had been filled with virtual people, virtual friends, and a virtual love story that seemed to have no happy ending and no conclusion.

She spent three days after she finished the book packing for England. She took winter clothes and favorite objects for the house. Some photographs of her father and small paintings that she wanted to hang in her bedroom. She took all of Winnie and Piglet's favorite toys and blankets. She had ten suitcases packed when she finished, which was the maximum she was allowed, paying for excess baggage, but it was easier than shipping it.

She looked around her house on the last night, sad to leave, and excited about the new adventure in England. She hadn't heard from Gray in nearly a week and wondered if he had fallen out of love with her. The dogs were restless that night, as though they knew something big was happening. She had hired a van to take her to the airport.

No one called her that night, and she wondered if she was doing the right thing going to England. She could always come home if it turned out to be a bad idea. Nothing was forever if you didn't want it to be. She wondered if Gray felt that way about her now, after a tortured summer battling with Matilda and bleeding money. It seemed like a high price to pay for love with a woman he barely knew.

She hadn't heard from him in days, and her imagination ran wild as she worried that he would give up on an excessively expensive divorce and stay married. Her mother's leaving her when she was a child had left her with abandonment issues, which surfaced now in full force. If he had decided not to go forward with the divorce, she wouldn't blame him, and she told herself that they'd both survive. At least they'd tried. She couldn't ask him for more than that.

And in his stressed-out state, Gray misjudged the situation and guessed that Sabrina would rather have no news than the daily reports that nothing had changed or been settled, that Matilda hadn't signed. He was trying to spare Sabrina, who assumed that the silences meant disaster and his love for her was waning. And late at night, she assumed the worst and panicked and barely slept.

She checked her computer at midnight and found an email from Felicity Parker-Smythe, her British publisher. Felicity wanted Sabrina to appear on a big British talk show to publicize her new book in England that was coming out in two weeks, after she arrived. And she wanted to give a party for her.

Sabrina wrote back, agreeing to do the talk show, and said that she'd need some time to settle in before Felicity gave her a party, but she thanked her for the thought. She wasn't in the mood for a party. There was a short email from Olivia too. They had said a tearful goodbye that afternoon, and Olivia had wished her luck, and they had promised to call each other often.

Then she sat in her garden for a last time. It was cool, and fall was in the air. It was time for her to leave, to discover her new life in England. She had opened her arms to the opportunity and to Gray. She loved him and she had no idea how things would turn out. But did one ever? Look at Caleb, she reminded herself. He thought he had it all, happiness sewn up for a lifetime, and then it vanished. All you ever had was the moment you were in, with no certainty of what the next moment would bring.

She closed the door to the garden and locked it, so she wouldn't forget to in the morning. Then she climbed into her big comfortable bed for the last time with Winnie and Piglet. They were both snoring as she snuggled up to them. It was the bed where she and Gray had made love, and she wondered if he was waiting for her or hiding from her. She thought of sending him an email, but she had nothing to tell him either, except that she loved him and she was coming to England, and she didn't care anymore if the only job open to her in his life was as his mistress. Maybe it really didn't matter after all.

She fell asleep thinking of him, and knew none of the answers. She'd have to see what would happen when she got there. If happiness was a choice, she chose to be with him. She was going to tell him that when she saw him, if he called her. Sometimes she felt as though he was slipping quietly out of her life. She wondered if he had given up on her and was afraid to tell her. Anything was possible. Maybe he was exiting her life as suddenly as he had entered it.

Chapter 15

The alarm went off at six o'clock. She fed the dogs, went to take a shower, and dressed for the trip. Agnes had pulled strings with someone she knew at the airline, and Winnie was traveling as a service dog, so he could be in the cabin with her. Piglet was going in her pink travel bag. Sabrina had all the health certificates she needed for them in England. The van was coming for her at seven-fifteen. She'd answered all her emails the night before, and nothing had come in during the night. There was no word from Gray, again.

She heard a car come up her driveway at seven and come to a grinding stop. It was Olivia, come to say goodbye again and give her a last hug.

"Give 'em hell!" Olivia said as they hugged, and Sabrina

laughed. Olivia was a faithful friend. Sabrina would be back sometime in the next six months to spend time here, but first she had to build her new life in England and make it her own. This was the beginning of a new adventure and new chapters, and whatever the future held for her. She wasn't running from it, she was running to it, and if Gray had decided not to be part of her new life, she'd be sad, but she'd survive. She had survived harder blows than that in her life. Happiness was not only a choice, it was a gift.

"Don't forget to call me," Olivia said, as Sabrina climbed into the van after she locked the house and set the alarm.

"I'll try not to forget," Sabrina said with a grin. "And don't call me in the morning on FaceTime, I look so ugly, I even scare myself."

There were tears in Olivia's eyes as she watched her go. Sabrina waved as the van drove away and turned onto the road, and disappeared. Sabrina's next adventure had begun.

Winnie and Piglet slept for most of the flight, Winnie at Sabrina's feet like a giant mop, and Piglet in her little bag. The older woman in the seat next to Sabrina looked concerned at the beginning of the flight and complimented her on how well-behaved the dogs were when they landed.

Sabrina got through customs with no problem, with all ten bags and the papers for the dogs. She hadn't texted Gray when she was arriving since she hadn't heard from him in several days, and she figured her arrival would be a disaster, between her luggage and the dogs. By the time she got through customs and immigration at Heathrow, the van and driver she'd ordered were waiting for her, and after walking Winnie and Piglet after the long flight, they set off for the last leg of the trip. It was eight o'clock and a balmy night. The sky was full of stars, which she hoped was a good sign. She felt as though she was flying through space on the drive, uncertain what she'd hear from Gray when she arrived. Anything was possible; good news, bad news, maybe he'd gone back to his wife and was waiting to tell Sabrina when she arrived. Maybe that was why she hadn't heard from him. She tried not to think about it on the drive. The dogs had gone back to sleep in the van after she walked them, and it was two hours later when they arrived at the familiar gates and drove through them to the house. Margaret was there waiting for her, even though it was late. She had tea sandwiches waiting, a pot of tea, and scones.

It was exciting to be there, and Sabrina couldn't wait to unpack the next day and put her familiar things around. She couldn't see the lake in the dark, but there were flowers from the garden around the house. Margaret went up to Sabrina's bedroom with her to make sure that everything was the way she wanted it, and then she left and went home, and Sabrina walked around with the dogs still on their leashes, so they wouldn't wander off and get lost in the house. She took them on another walk after she ate some of the sandwiches, and smiled as she looked around. It was exciting to think that this was her home now. She couldn't wait to take them on a long walk the next day.

They went back inside, and up to her bedroom. Winnie was sniffing everywhere, and Piglet wanted to be carried, so Sabrina held her, and took off their leashes and closed the doors of the master suite.

"We're home, guys," she said as they stared at her, and she took their favorite blankets out of the one bag she'd brought upstairs. It had her nightgown, and their favorite toys, some sweaters and jeans, and her toiletries, everything she needed for the night. She looked out the window at the moon and the stars. It was a beautiful night. A perfect night to come home. And also a strange feeling, knowing that Gray was there somewhere, not far away, unless he was in London. She didn't know. She wanted to send him a message to tell him she was there, but she was going to wait to hear from him. He knew when she was coming, and the next move was up to him now. They hadn't seen each other in over three months, which felt like an eternity, and she had no idea what he was going to say to her.

The dogs were looking at her expectantly, as though they

weren't sure what to do next or why they were there. She lifted Piglet onto the bed, and Winnie climbed up next to her and lay down cautiously, not sure if he was supposed to be there. Sabrina washed her face and brushed her teeth in the giant old-fashioned bathroom and changed into her nightgown. She wandered into the little study where she was going to write. She hadn't unpacked her computer yet and was going to do it in the morning. Then she went back to the bedroom and turned off all the lights except the one next to her bed, so she wouldn't get confused if she woke up, but the moon was shining brightly into the room. Winnie let out a little whimper as he stretched out on the bed, and she patted him, as Piglet snuggled next to her, and then climbed onto her to make sure Sabrina wasn't going anywhere.

Sabrina lay there for a long time, thinking of Gray, wondering where he was and what was happening. She just had to let him be, until he reached out to her. He would eventually, whatever he had to say. It was comforting knowing that he was nearby now. She could almost feel him, and whatever had happened would be the outcome that was meant to be.

She reached for her phone on the night table and sent Olivia a text. "Safely arrived." The answer came back two minutes later, "Good luck." It was comforting feeling that someone cared where she was.

She and the two dogs huddled close together in the unfamiliar bed and fell asleep. When Sabrina woke in the morning, the sun was streaming into the room and it was nine o'clock, and the dogs were waiting to go out. She put her coat on over her nightgown, put on her shoes, and ran down the stairs with them, opened the front door and took them out. There were already gardeners working in the flowerbeds, and they smiled when they saw her with Winnie and Piglet.

"Morning, your Ladyship," they said, and she smiled. She didn't feel like a Ladyship in her ragtag outfit and tangled hair, but that's who she was here. And then Margaret came to find her and asked her what she'd like for breakfast, and she said that coffee and toast would be fine.

When they went back in, she fed the dogs, and spent the morning unpacking. Margaret helped with some of it, and Sabrina put the photographs of her father in the library downstairs. She had brought him home.

She hung the paintings in her bedroom, filled some of the closets in the dressing room with her clothes, and set up her desk. And when she finished, she showered and dressed and then took Winnie and Piglet for a long walk to the lake. She carried Piglet in her little carrier, and Winnie raced back and forth, ecstatic with all the space he suddenly had. He looked as though he knew he was home. All he needed was a flock of sheep to herd.

Sabrina stopped in Caragh's secret garden and talked to her out loud.

"Well, I'm back, wish me luck." And then she walked back to the house. Winnie tried to wade into the lake and she called him back, and he came running to her with wet paws and Piglet barked at him.

She left them with Margaret when she got back, and borrowed one of the staff cars to drive into the village to look around again. She really did feel like she'd come home. She knew she had made the right decision, whatever happened next with Gray. On the way back, she saw the gates to the dower house she remembered, pulled off the road, cautiously rang the guardian's bell, and asked if Mr. Abbott was at home. She knew Gray would be at work in the city, but she wanted to say hello to his father. The guardian was back in a few minutes and told her that Mr. Abbott would be pleased to see her, and she ran up the steps to the front door, and the housekeeper let her in. She found him in the library where she'd met him before.

Phillip Abbott stood up tall and straight as she walked in and greeted her with a warm smile.

"You're back!" He looked delighted to see her and surprisingly well. "When did you arrive?" If he knew something was amiss with Gray, it didn't show.

"Last night. I'm sorry to just drop in, but I wanted to say

hello. I was trying to get my bearings and drove to the village, and I stopped here on the way back."

"Be careful what side of the road you're on," he said with concern. But she had mastered it before.

"You look very well," Sabrina said, and he really did. Surprisingly so.

"Gray took wonderful care of me. He's living here now, you know. He doesn't trust me on my own!" He offered her tea and she declined. "Does Gray know you've arrived?" She shook her head.

"I think he's been very busy. He knows I was coming in this week. I'm sure I'll hear from him when he has time," she said discreetly, as Phillip searched her eyes, and reached out to touch her hand.

"I'm sure you'll hear from him soon. I think he's finishing what he's been doing." She nodded, and he hugged her before she left, and then he sat pensively, thinking about her. There was something very special and unusual about her, and he could understand why his son was so taken with her. He wasn't sure if he should tell Gray he'd seen her or not. He didn't want to interfere. He knew how difficult the past three months had been for him, and he thought it best to leave the timing of their meeting up to him. Destiny had its own plan.

Sabrina didn't hear from Gray that night or the next day,

as she settled in. She met all the gardeners and rode Rupert's horse again. She got a text from Caleb, who said he was arriving the following week. Felicity confirmed her appearance on the talk show in ten days. Sabrina was starting a life here and feeling at home. She decided to spend the night in London before the talk show, and made a reservation at Claridge's. She wondered if Caleb would be there then too. She wanted him to come to see the manor house if he had time.

She assumed that Gray's father must have told Gray that she'd come by, and she took the three days of silence afterwards as a bad sign. If he had good news, he would have called her or come to see her, and he didn't. She had to make the best of it anyway and knew she couldn't let it stop her. This was her home now, with or without him. Her happiness here couldn't depend on him. If it was bad news, she'd hear it soon enough. His silence for over a week said it all. She had heard nothing from him in at least ten days. She knew the talk show would distract her, and Caleb's visit would warm her. She had a friend here. She wasn't counting on Gray to entertain her or keep her busy or make her happy. And whether he still loved her or not, she knew who she was and that she belonged here. Her uncle had determined that, and no one could take that away from her now, whether they loved her or not. She no longer cringed when people used her title. It had begun to sound normal in a matter of days. Winnie and Piglet acted as though they owned the place. They followed Margaret everywhere, hoping to be fed.

Sabrina had been there for five days when she finally had a text from Gray. All it said was, "I know you must be here. I'll be with you soon." He didn't sign it or say he loved her or explain, and the first sentence suggested to her that his father hadn't told him about her visit. He was leaving them to their own devices. They were old enough to work it out for themselves. Whatever Gray was doing, he wasn't ready to see her, and she kept busy on the estate, driving around, meeting people, and visiting the farms. She had never expected to be as happy here as she was. She felt as though she belonged here, and really had come home. Even without seeing Gray, everything about it felt right.

It was another three days before she heard from Gray again. Two dozen roses arrived with a note. All it said was, "May I see you tomorrow?" It sounded both distant and formal at the same time. The roses were beautiful, and she wasn't sure if they meant hello or goodbye. But whichever it was, he wanted to tell her to her face. She wasn't looking forward to bad news in person, if it was, but she felt an obligation to be dignified and brave and see him. She owed him at least that since she had turned his life upside down with the standards she had set. She felt guilty about it now.

She shouldn't have expected him to turn his life around for her. What right did she have? But she had a right to set the values she believed in for herself. She was only sorry if what she had wanted had hurt him, and she was sure now it had. She wrote back as simply as he had written to her. "Yes. When?"

He texted back, "Is six o'clock too late?"

And she answered. "No. Fine. See you then."

She tried not to think about it that night, and used her study for the first time. She had an essay to write for a magazine and wrote it that night. She got up early the next morning and went for a long walk. She took Winnie with her, and left Piglet at home with Margaret, curled up in one of the beds she brought with her and put in the kitchen.

She thought about the meeting with Gray. She didn't expect it to be good news now. It had been too long. He would have delivered good news as soon as he knew she'd arrived. He would have come rushing over and taken her in his arms and told her. She'd been there for over a week now. She remembered what they'd told each other, that whatever came would be the right answer, and they'd be happy in future anyway. They weren't at the mercy of other people's decisions, or each other's. Sabrina had been through loss before, and disappointment and heartbreak. They were familiar to her and she knew she could survive them, and still find happiness in what was left. She didn't want Gray to have that kind of power over her, nor did she want that kind of power over him, to ruin his life. He couldn't spoil her happiness here. Her uncle had given all of this to her as a gift, to thrive in and enjoy, not to mourn what she had lost in the past and couldn't have now. Happiness really was a choice, and whatever Gray's explanation now, or his reason, it didn't matter. She had to make her own happiness, as she always had, and would again. She would have liked to contribute to his happiness if she had been able to, but the die had been cast long since.

She was quiet that afternoon, and dressed before she saw him. She didn't want to look a mess when he came. At least he could remember her looking dignified and respectable, and whatever happened, whatever he did or said, she told herself she couldn't cry. She could cry later, after he left. She wanted to keep it short.

Sabrina thought of her mother as she got ready, and how beaten she had looked, how bitter she was about life, how empty she was as a human being, and she never wanted to be that person. Simone thought life had cheated her, but she had cheated herself and missed the best part. Sabrina's father had mourned forever two women he wasn't destined to have. If Gray Abbott wasn't her destiny, then she wouldn't mourn him. She would wish him well, release him, and free him to the life he chose, and his destiny. You couldn't hold on to what you didn't have and were never meant to. She remembered a phrase from the Bible: "Loose him and let him go." She would try to do that when she saw Gray, no matter how hard. It was the last gift she could give him, and the hardest. His liberty, with her blessing and her love. The loss wouldn't diminish her, it would make her better and stronger.

She looked serious when she came downstairs in a black skirt and plain white sweater and high heels.

She was sitting in the library when she heard him drive up. He banged the knocker, and she got up to answer it. Margaret had already gone home. Winnie and Piglet were asleep in her room. They were exhausted by the end of the day from all the running around they did. She looked beautiful and solemn when she opened the door, and for a minute, he took her breath away. She forgot sometimes how strikingly handsome he was. It was a nice bonus, but it wasn't what she loved most about him. He had come straight from the office and was wearing a dark suit. She was glad she had changed clothes for him, and didn't look a mess, wearing an old shirt and jeans, as she wore when she visited the farms. She'd met all the farmers now, and their wives. It was an important part of what Rupert had left her, and a responsibility she took seriously,

Gray looked startled when he saw her, and didn't know what to say for a minute.

"Hello. You look beautiful."

"Hello. So do you." She stepped aside so he could come in. "Would you like some wine?"

"Sure." He followed her into the kitchen. She'd had Margaret bring up two bottles from the wine cellar, red and white, and she'd left an opener on the table. "How does it feel being here?" he asked her, with a gentle look in his eyes.

"Wonderful," she said, as he opened a bottle of red wine, poured two glasses, and handed one to her. She felt shy with him now, after his long silence.

"I'm glad." He smiled at her. "My father loved your visit, by the way. He didn't tell me you'd come to see him until I told him last night I was seeing you today. I think he doesn't want to interfere."

"I guessed that he hadn't told you, from your text."

"Why didn't you tell me when you arrived?" he asked her, as he took the bottle and they headed toward the library and sat down. It was a cozy room with floor-to-ceiling old books with beautiful bindings.

"I figured you were busy, and you'd get in touch with me when you were ready to. I know it's been crazy for you lately."

He smiled. "That's an understatement. I think World War Two must have been easier. It's been a learning experience," he said, and relaxed a little with the wine. They were watching each other closely, with a thousand unspoken words between them. Words that might never be said. "I'm sorry I haven't written to you much lately. The news was so grim for a while, I didn't have the heart to. I didn't want to keep writing you bad news. I kept hoping it would turn around. I didn't want to write to you until I had something concrete to say. I didn't want you to think that I wasn't doing anything or that I didn't care. It just got very intense."

"I can imagine," she said quietly. "I'm sorry I put you through it. I had no right to."

"You didn't put me through it," he corrected her quickly. "You set a standard for yourself, which you had every right to do. I put you in a bad spot right from the beginning, by not giving you the lay of the land right away."

"It's a standard that probably doesn't make much sense in today's world. By our age, people have attachments and obligations and responsibilities, and history. I could hardly expect you to be unattached."

"If I were American, I'd have been divorced years ago, which would have been a lot simpler, and I should have done it then. Even my father thought so, it turns out. And he says mother did too. Matilda and I were probably the worst-suited couple on the planet. I knew it pretty quickly, but I thought I was supposed to stick with it anyway. So we broke all the rules, and lied to ourselves and each other for another twenty or twenty-five years. Having the kids was a good distraction, but sooner or later the mess is so big there's no way to fix it. It takes guts to get out of it. Most of our marriage was a lie. The biggest lie of all was that we liked each other. We weren't even friends. So, whatever happens now, you did me a favor, Sabrina. Matilda and I would have imploded sooner or later. We've been heading toward a brick wall for years."

"Thank you for being nice about it. I felt so guilty for all the money I was costing you." It felt good to say it now, and at least they were both saying how they'd felt. It helped to clear the air.

"You didn't cost me a fortune, she did. Less of a fortune than she would have liked, but enough. That was my fault too. If I had dealt with it earlier, it wouldn't have been as expensive. But I had a good lawyer, and in the end, he negotiated a decent deal. She's not thrilled, but she should be. I gave her the house and a very healthy amount to live on. And once we got started, I realized that it wasn't about you. It was about how unhappy we'd both been, and how bitter she was about it. We both created the mess by never facing it. That had nothing to do with you. If I'd stayed married to her, it would only have gotten worse. You helped me escape a prison of my own making. You were right. It was a choice. We both chose to stay in it, knowing how bad it was, and how wrong. No matter what it cost me, I'm a free man now. Whatever I do next will be a choice too. Hopefully a better choice than I made before." He smiled at her as he said it, and he really did look happy. She felt a huge weight lift off her shoulders. She had felt so guilty and responsible for the trouble and expense she had caused him. "What about you? Where are you in all this now? I was so busy trying to get out of jail, I hadn't been paying proper attention to you, and I apologize for that. I didn't want to say another word to you until I could tell you I was free."

"When I didn't hear from you, I thought maybe you had gone back to her, or had given up the idea of divorcing her. I didn't want to press you about it. I figured you'd tell me sooner or later."

He smiled again. "I forget that imagination of yours and the kind of books you write. If this were one of your books, I'd have cut her up in little pieces and put her in a suitcase. I was negotiating with her every day. It was almost as grim and gory as one of your books, but not quite. And I was too upset to talk about it. But there was never even the remotest possibility of my going back to her. Not for a minute. I was so busy being mad at her, I forgot to tell you that I love you. I assumed you knew. I was an idiot, I guess. I don't multitask well. I can't be in a rage at one woman while telling another woman I love her. I had to put you on pause, and I wanted to be sure I could get out of it before I came to you cleanly, finally, and offered myself to you."

"In the last few weeks, I thought you'd changed your mind," she said softly. He looked horrified when she said it.

"So then what happened? You met someone else? You have a boyfriend? You got engaged? You're married?" He looked shaken even though he tried to make a joke of it. It had never occurred to him that she would think he'd changed his mind about her if he didn't write to her.

"No, actually," she said. "I'm still free."

"And you still came over here to take your rightful place, on the estate that belongs to you. At least that's something," he said, relieved.

"I learned that lesson from my parents. They both deprived themselves of everything that was worth having. I decided not to do that. One of those choices again."

"And the right one in this case. You belong here, Sabrina."

"I know that now," she said peacefully. "I felt it the minute I got back. Winnie and Piglet seem to think so too. Winnie even found some sheep to herd on one of the farms yesterday. He came home covered in mud, absolutely thrilled. He didn't do as well with the goats, but the sheep were right up his alley." Gray grinned at her description of it.

"I'm glad you're happy here. It would have been so wrong if you'd sold it. You can still have your barn in the Berkshires, but you need to be here, at least some of the time."

"I know I do. I want to be."

"I seem to be living here for the moment too," he said. "I gave Matilda the house, so for now I'm living with my father. It's good for him, and it's good for me too. He gave me a hell of a scare, but he's better than ever now. And I love staying with him. But it's a hellish commute. Once I'm sure he's really all right again and not falling down the stairs, I need to find a flat in London. The commute is going to kill me." He looked at her seriously then. "We signed the final agreement this morning. That's why you didn't hear from me until yesterday. I wanted to know that was done before I saw you. The agreement is final. We'll be divorced in a year. And now that we've established that you don't have a boyfriend, a fiancé, or a new husband since I got too distracted to write to you, where does that leave us now? What do you want to do? I'm yours if you still want me," he said gently, reaching out a hand to her. She took it, and held his hand as tears filled her eyes.

"I thought you were coming to say goodbye to me tonight, and that the divorce wasn't possible, or you'd gone back to her." He left his seat then and went to sit next to her on the couch.

"That was never, ever remotely possible. You've been very brave," he said, and wiped the tears from her eyes. "We put up a hell of a fight, but it was every bit worth it, so I could come to you free and clear the way it should have been from the beginning. You're an honorable woman, Lady Brooks, and you don't deserve anything less than that." He kissed her then. It had been a long road back to each other, and she'd been ready to give him up because she loved him. He had fought for her because he loved her. She'd been bold enough to make the choice for happiness. And they were brave enough to love each other. "I'm never letting you go, you know. You'll be stuck with me forever," he warned her.

"I think I can live with that." She smiled at him. "I'll get back to you on that."

"The hell you will," he said, and held her tight in his arms. "Oh, and by the way, my father sent you this," he said, and pulled a small round black velvet box out of his pocket. The box looked very old. She held it cautiously, and looked at Gray, and he opened it for her. It was a beautiful cushion-cut diamond in a simple antique setting. "It's my mother's engagement ring. My father wants you to have it. He told me to put it on your finger before you come to your senses and get away from me." He took it out of the box then and slipped it on her finger. It fit perfectly. All she could do was stare at it and look at him, and she was laughing through her tears. "You have to stop crying, Sabrina. I'm sure it's not respectable to get engaged while you're waiting for a divorce to come through, but I don't give a damn."

"You're crazy and I love you," she said happily. Loving him

and coming to England to claim her rightful place were the best choices she had ever made.

"We'll be crazy together. Come and see my father now. He wants to see the ring on you." It looked gorgeous on her hand as she stood up with him and he kissed her again. "I'm going to have to make some arrangements for my father. Because until I do, I can't spend the nights with you," he said, as they walked to the front door together with his arm around her.

"Winnie will be happy to hear it," she said, smiling as she looked at her hand. She had thought tonight was goodbye, and instead it was the beginning.

"I will sleep with a Chihuahua, but I will not sleep with a sheepdog. We'll get him his own bed."

"That'll do," she said, as they closed the front door behind them.

"You will sleep with me before the divorce comes through, won't you?" he said with a look of panic.

"Now that we're engaged, I suppose I will."

"You'd damn well better," he said, as she laughed and they got into his Aston Martin to drive down the road to see his father, who was waiting for them with a bottle of champagne.

The choice for happiness and a full life had been a good one, for all of them. It had taken courage for both of them.

Chapter 16

Gray stayed at Claridge's with Sabrina when she went to London to appear on the talk show to plug her new book. The appearance went well, and he went to the studio with her, and to his office afterwards. Caleb called her right after the show.

"I just got to London last night, and I saw you on the show this morning. You were terrific, Sabrina. And what is that thing I saw on your left hand? It almost blinded me," he said in his elegant southern drawl, and she laughed.

"I'm engaged," she said proudly.

"Damn. I knew it. I thought it was some kind of flashlight you were holding."

"It's his mother's engagement ring."

"And I haven't even hit the year mark yet. Timing is

everything. I guess it wasn't our destiny." He was teasing her when he said it, but there was also truth to it. "I'm happy for you, Sabrina," he said seriously. "I have a feeling you made the right choice this time."

"I know I did. I want you to meet him, and you have to come out and see us at Brooks Manor."

"I will, as soon as I get a break in our shooting schedule. You take care now. I'll call you. And congratulations to the lucky guy." She felt lucky too after she talked to him. Caleb was a lovely man, and he was going to be a wonderful friend.

Danielle Steel

Have you liked Danielle Steel on Facebook?

Be the first to know about Danielle's latest books, access exclusive competitions and stay in touch with news about Danielle.

www.facebook.com/DanielleSteelOfficial

SECOND ACT

As head of a prestigious movie studio, Andy Westfield has had every conceivable professional luxury. The son of Hollywood royalty, he always put his career before his marriage, and now, besides his daughter and young grand-children, it's the only thing he truly loves.

But then Andy's world is upended. The studio is sold, and the buyer's son demands the top seat. Andy's world spirals. He knows he needs to get as far away from LA as possible until the dust settles and he can find a new way forward.

Andy signs a six-month rental for a luxurious home in a small town on the English coast and hires a local woman to help get his affairs in order. A former journalist, Violet Smith is at a crossroads too. But when Violet leaves the manuscript of her unfinished novel behind after work one day, Andy lets his curiosity get the best of him and is captivated by a story that begs to be adapted for the big screen. Could this be the miracle they've both been looking for?

Coming soon

PURE STEEL. PURE HEART.

About the Author

Danielle Steel has been hailed as one of the world's most popular authors, with a billion copies of her novels sold. Her recent international bestsellers include *Palazzo, The Wedding Planner* and *Worthy Opponents*. She is also the author of *His Bright Light*, the story of her son Nick Traina's life and death; *A Gift of Hope*, a memoir of her work with the homeless; and the children's books *Pretty Minnie in Paris* and *Pretty Minnie in Hollywood*. Danielle divides her time between Paris and her home in northern California.